# Legends of the Northern Paiute

## AS TOLD BY WILSON WEWA

Maggie Wewa. Photo by Cynthia D. Stowell, from *Faces of a Reservation* (Oregon Historical Society Press, 1989).

# Legends of the Northern Paiute

## AS TOLD BY WILSON WEWA

Compiled and edited
and with an introduction by

## JAMES A. GARDNER

Oregon State University Press   Corvallis

Library of Congress Cataloging-in-Publication Data

Names: Wewa, Wilson, author. | Gardner, James A., compiler, editor.
Title: Legends of the Northern Paiute / as told by Wilson Wewa ; compiled
    and edited and with an introduction by James A. Gardner.
Description: Corvallis : Oregon State University Press, 2017. | Includes
    bibliographical references.
Identifiers: LCCN 2017028005 | ISBN 9780870719004 (trade paperback
    : alkaline paper)
Subjects: LCSH: Northern Paiute Indians—Folklore. | Legends—Great
    Basin. | Folklore—Great Basin. | Great Basin—Social life and customs. |
    BISAC: FICTION / Fairy Tales, Folk Tales, Legends & Mythology.
Classification: LCC E99.P2 W439 2017 | DDC 398.20897/4577—dc23
LC record available at https://lccn.loc.gov/2017028005

First published in 2017 by Oregon State University Press
Printed in the United States of America

Oregon State University Press
121 The Valley Library
Corvallis OR 97331-4501
541-737-3166 • fax 541-737-3170
www.osupress.oregonstate.edu

# Contents

# Editor's Introduction

Several years ago I attended a lecture by Wilson Wewa at an Oregon Archaeology Celebration series program at Smith Rock State Park in Terrebonne, Oregon. At the time, I was researching and writing about the Native American and settler history of Central Oregon and the Northern Great Basin. Within that context I had interviewed Wilson about the Northern Paiutes. A spiritual leader and oral historian of the tribe, Wilson is also a great-great grandson of both Chief Paulina and Chief Weahwewa, two of the most important and influential Paiute chiefs in the tribe's history.[1] Wilson is a wellspring of Northern Paiute oral history, storytelling, and tribal legends, most of which he learned from his grandmother and tribal elders. For years he has told these histories and legends on the Warm Springs Reservation, a confederated reservation of the Wasco, Tenino, and Northern Paiute tribes in Central Oregon—and the home of Wilson and his family. Wilson also shares this legacy in Paiute ceremonies and burials and, on occasion, at academic seminars and classes.

That evening at Smith Rock, Wilson told several Paiute legends that were entirely new to me. When his talk was over I thanked him for his presentation and inquired whether the legends he had shared had ever been recorded and saved, or if there was a risk that they could be lost to history. Wilson responded that these legends were neither recorded nor written, and that he was deeply concerned that they would be lost with his passing. He expressed a strong desire to preserve the legends for future generations and to promote a broader public understanding. With that conversation, our collaboration of many years began, and this book is one of its results.

As Wilson explains in his engaging foreword to this book, his grandmother, Maggie Wewa, was the principal source of the original Paiute legends he shares here, and he has warmly dedicated this book to her. Historian Cynthia Stowell has written about Maggie Wewa's love of traditional Paiute stick game gambling and how much she enjoyed traveling to tournaments all over the Northern Great Basin: "You feel good when you go to a different place," she said, "instead of like a prisoner." Wilson often went along with his grandmother, traveling by bus or later in Wilson's pickup. He tells many engaging stories of those years and trips. Stowell also published a photograph of what she calls Maggie Wewa's "striking Paiute face," and that photograph is reprinted at the beginning of this book.[2]

My favorite research experience with Wilson was a field trip we made to the Malheur Cave, south of Burns, Oregon. There, in oceans of sagebrush surrounded by the vast, rugged, treeless, and windswept terrain of the Great Basin, we found the mouth of the very cave that is the setting for the first legend of this collection, "The Creation Story and the Malheur Cave." On the day we visited, Wilson burned a sage offering at the entrance before entering the cave for a time of respectful reflection and prayer. That trip was an especially enjoyable and insightful journey into the heart of the Paiute homeland, and Paiute history and legends.

Most of the storytelling, recording, and review of these legends occurred at my home at Ranch at the Canyons during the winter—the Paiute storytelling season. Wilson and I have always been committed to preserving the legends in his own words. In traditional Paiute legends, the setting and the storytelling were integral parts of each story, so we labored mightily to also preserve as much as possible of the spirit, humor, surprise, cadence, and verve of these legends.

Our lively and sustained collaboration eventually yielded this collection of original and never-before-published Northern Paiute legends. As much as this collection was created for the future, these legends are deeply rooted in the past, in the rich history and culture of the Northern Paiutes. For too long, their tribal history has been little researched and poorly understood. But recent research, teaching, and writing about the Northern Paiutes—including my own, and that of my students and teachers at the University of Oregon—are welcome correctives.

For thousands of years the Northern Paiutes lived in the vast and rugged high desert environment of the Northern Great Basin and developed a distinct culture well-adapted to their environment. At the time of contact with Euro-American traders and explorers, there were perhaps seventy-five hundred Paiutes spread across the Great Basin—hunting, gathering, and fishing in some twenty-one bands, each with its own name, territory, chief, and spiritual leader, but no overarching tribal government. Their lives were marked by sociability and cooperation in hunting and gathering and in all aspects of their family and band lives, as well as in warfare, treaties, and major tribal events. Not surprisingly, the Northern Paiutes lived predominantly around the region's many sources of water, including the Deschutes, John Day, Powder, Burnt, Malheur, and Owyhee river basins of the Northern Great Basin, and the innumerable tributaries that feed those streams. Although continuously challenged by their harsh high desert environment, the Paiute had access to vast land and water and grazing and fishery resources.

Legends have always been an integral element of Paiute culture. Their legends—lively, insightful, ribald, and often humorous—emphasize and reinforce Paiute social bonds through a compelling mixture of entertainment and education, and serve as a vital source of continuity for tribal ways. In the process, the legends reaffirm and pass along important tribal values, even as they warned of draconian penalties for any breach or flouting of those values.

There is considerable consensus among the tribes of the Confederated Warm Springs Reservation that important elements of tribal life and culture are much diminished on the reservation today, and in other Northern Paiute communities in the western United States—at Burns and Fort McDermitt Reservations in Oregon, Pyramid Lake and the Walker River Reservations in Nevada and Duck Valley Reservations in Nevada and Idaho, and elsewhere. In particular, many elements of Paiute history, culture, and legends have been eroded because of the traumatic and tragic native history of American invasion, warfare, land taking, and forced removal from native homelands. Not surprisingly, Paiute language and legends have been and are being lost, too. Wilson Wewa's concern about this cultural loss has provided the impetus for our subsequent collaboration and endeavors to gather and preserve what we could of Paiute history and legends.

We urge the reader to be open to the vitality of these legends as told by a renowned Paiute storyteller to a village group gathered around a campfire during the storytelling season of a cold and clear winter night in the Northern Great Basin. Enjoy these legends as they were told, out loud, and full of conviction, emphasis, lilt, pause, and humor. Read them envisioning the storyteller as a vital part of the story, because that is how these legends took form and have been told over thousands of years.

I am especially appreciative of Wilson Wewa for his extraordinary storytelling skills and sharing, and his dedicated attention in recording and reviewing these legends for publication. These legends are a joy to hear told—and sometimes sung. Along the way, we have built a friendship based on collaboration and shared interests and objectives. Through this sustained multicultural cooperation we have accomplished more together than either of us could have produced alone. Thanks also to the Paiute tribal elders for supporting Wilson's storytelling and the saving and sharing of these original legends.

I also appreciate others who have helped in this process, including in particular Gloria Colvin, who Wilson affectionately calls "the church lady." She has been part of this project since it started, and her participation has always reflected her affection for the legends and cultures of Native Americans. I want to warmly thank Julie O'Neal of my office for her invaluable assistance in the preparation and review of these legends for publication.

Finally, I would like to thank Ms. Mary Elizabeth Braun and the Oregon State University Press for their support in the preparation and publication of this book. I also appreciate the longstanding OSU Press commitment to scholarly publications relating to Indigenous and Native American Studies—including the important and often neglected Northern Paiutes of the Northern Great Basin.

This project provides a unique window into the roots and character of the Northern Paiute tribe and culture. Wilson Wewa and I are pleased to help bring these original Northern Paiute legends into the sunlight of publication, and to enhance tribal and public understanding of this Paiute legacy.

*James A. Gardner*
*Ranch at the Canyons, Terrebonne*

1. Because the Weahwewa family name was difficult for English-speakers to pronounce, it was eventually shortened to Wewa.

2. Image of Maggie Wewa, in Cynthia D. Stowell, *Faces of a Reservation, A Portrait of the Warm Springs Indian Reservation* (Portland, Oregon Historical Society Press, 1987) 36.

# Acknowledgments and Dedication

I am indebted to many people who have contributed to the making of this book of Northern Paiute legends and stories. Since the time of traveling with my grandparents, to the time when all those Paiute elders followed *Nuwupo*, Milky Way, it is impossible to remember each and every one that contributed to this work.

As a little boy, it was at the root camp in southeastern Oregon that I was first introduced to stories of my people. It was not in the formal teacher-student fashion of school, but in the relaxed seminomadic fashion of the old days. Now, it is my intention to continue using modern modes of communication to ensure that these stories will never fade away.

Throughout the Great Basin, it was the many rodeos, pow-wows, handgame tournaments, and funerals that were the catalyst that brought Grandma and I into contact with many of the friends I found among the old people. I enjoyed sitting at their tables, at the woodshed, and in their cars or under the trees where I heard parts of stories and legends, and in some cases the full legend or story.

My loving thanks go to the Paiute and Shoshone elders of the Duck Valley Reservation. I enjoyed listening to Douglas and Clara Little, Willie Pretty, Eva George, Lillie Little, Benny Tom, Lena Black, and the great grandson of Chief Egan, Hubert Egan, and his wife, Elaine.

I offer my deep appreciation to the elders of the Fort McDermitt Reservation. The songs and stories that I learned from Minnie Curtis, Art and Ethel Cavanaugh, Donald Barr and his wife, and never to forget the Paiute statesman and keeper of tradition, Oren George, who taught me the Paiute burial songs and traditional stories relating to the Milky Way.

I will always remember the elders who welcomed me onto the Pyramid Lake Reservation and who trusted me to drive them to the pine nut picking and to gather buckberries, while telling their stories, lifeways, and growing up stories, and the laughter of the many translations of what was happening in the story. I will never forget Bill and Nina Smith, Art and Mavis Dunn, Virginia Barlese, Lorraine Wadsworth, Freda Sam, Emmy Lowery, Flora Green, Davey Christy, Simon John, and Ralph Burns. I am most indebted to Myra Whitney, the daughter of a *Nuwu Puhagum* (traditional healer). It was Myra who translated the stories for me to remember.

My immeasurable appreciation goes to the elders of the small community of Fort Bidwell, California: Clarence DeGarmo, Jimmy Washo, Rose Townsend, and the matriarch Nettie Degarmo, who caught a ride home with Grandma Maggie and me on a few occasions after a successful hand game weekend.

Last but not least, my uncle and aunt, Andy and Bea Allen, Popeye and Mary McCloud, and Wesley Dick and Frances Sam, who shared renditions of the stories as they were told at Shurz, Nevada, on the Walker River Reservation. Andy enjoyed telling his tales during the Pinenut Festival year after year.

I will certainly miss someone and it is not intentional. These stories are worth remembering and the sincerest thanks go to all my people who supported me by encouraging me to go forward with this book.

My biggest inspiration was from my elders on the Burns Paiute Reservation, who said, "If you don't do it, how will our people learn." To Rena Beers, Agnes Phillips, Marion Louis, Maude Stanley, Hanna Charles, and the first orator I ever listened to, Davey Jim: thank you.

This list would not be complete without acknowledging my grandma, Maggie Wewa, who now knows that I have completed this work, for the many hours we traveled and the repetitive stories and history that she shared and the geographical features she named in Paiute, and especially for opening the doors to meet all these wonderful elders and storytellers. Grandma, I am most indebted to you for the love and patience you had with my inquiries to know more. Without your warm-hearted sharing of your life story and the relationships of our Great Basin people, I would not be in a position to help keep these legends of our people alive for future generations.

And to my great friend and collaborator, Jim Gardner, who so long ago asked me, "Wilson, have you ever thought about writing down all these stories?" and then said, "Let's make it happen!" Well, here are the fruits of our labors. I can't forget Gloria Colvin, who encouraged and continued to ask for clarification on the meanings of the stories and offered her insights to editing each and every legend. To both of you I owe a debt of gratitude for helping me write this book in a more clear and concise way.

In closing, there are many stories and legends that are the same, yet different, depending on who is telling them through oral tradition, and on how they came out through the storyteller, the one interpreting them. I have tried to the best of my ability to capture the essence of that tradition. I will never say this is the only way, but it is the way I heard them and will always remember them.

My continued admiration and recognition will be transmitted to all those past Paiute people who shared their remembrances, knowledge, and information through these stories, and to their children, grandchildren, and those yet to come.

May our Creator guide those who choose to recapture the past by following the paths these stories bring you to and to be inspired to continue this tradition.

*Preface and Personal History*

## Growing up in "Hollywood" on the Warm Springs Reservation

My name is Wilson Wewa. I was born in Central Oregon and lived all of my life on the Warm Springs Indian Reservation. As I grew up there was a lot of change occurring on the reservation. The neighborhood I grew up in was called "Hollywood." In our community a dirt road ran through a big ravine, and there were lots of houses up and down the length of that ravine.

In those days I didn't think we were poor people. But later on I heard people say that poor people live in Hollywood. That made me think. I think that is why they used to call it Hollywood, as a way to make fun of the people that lived there.

I grew up there all my young days. We didn't have electricity. We didn't have running water. We didn't have indoor plumbing. And there were only four or five faucets that serviced that entire area for a quarter of a mile. Everybody used to go out with their buckets to get water and bring it to their homes. In the winter time, they used to make a fire next to the faucet so it wouldn't freeze up. Most of the people had wood stoves, and most of the people had outhouses. So that's the way I grew up, and I grew up in that kind of time. But I didn't think we were poor.

My dad worked hard all his life to provide for us. I had two brothers and two sisters, and they were all younger than I was. My mom was Eugenia Wolf. My dad, Wilson Wewa Sr., was from Warm Springs. He was a full-blooded Paiute and grew up on the south end of the reservation. My grandma and grandpa, Maggie and Sam Wewa, had a ranch on the south end of the reservation in an area called Seekseequa. Their ranch was right across from Round Butte, and they had horses and cattle. So my dad grew up in that time and place.

My brothers and sisters and I liked to go out to our grandma and grandpa's house to visit, because being out there was far away from Warm Springs. At that time, in the fifties, the community was probably one tenth of the size it is now. But we liked to go stay with our grandma and grandpa. That's where all of our saddle horses were. So we were able to ride there. Also, my dad had a brother and a sister, and their children were often up there, too. It was good to go up there and visit, because we were able to see our cousins, and play and crawl around on the rocks, and play in the juniper thickets, and go down in the canyon—things I wouldn't let my nieces, nephews, and grandchildren do today! We would be gone all day, playing.

There were times when we'd hear the frying pan being hit with a spoon. My grandma would do that. We would come running back to the house, because it was lunchtime.

We learned how to take care of horses on the ranch. Our family was always around horses. And that's where we learned how to take care of horses, and I learned how to ride. We all learned how to ride when we were little, probably five or six years old and already riding horses. We had no problem riding bareback, without a saddle. Some of our horses were tame enough that we could put a rope over their noses and ride with that rope on their noses, and without a bridle—even galloping or racing across the field on them! That's how we grew up at that time.

I didn't think we were poor. We always had food on our table. Our dad made sure of that. He had cattle and horses, but that didn't provide a good living all the time. So my dad worked on building the regulating dam on the Deschutes River. Then he worked on building the Pelton Dam. And he worked on building the Round Butte Dam. When those were finished he worked in the Warm Springs lumber mill. Then he started working in the woods as a tree faller. He worked all of his life trying to take care of us and get us through school.

He always used to tell us that it was important for us to have an education. Like a lot of people in Central Oregon, he only went to school through the sixth grade. That's as far as he went, the sixth grade. He wanted us to do better than that. So he would always tell us to study hard and not to miss school. So that's what he told us. My older cousins all ended up going to boarding school in Warm Springs. Warm Springs had a boarding school, and some of those brick buildings are still standing.

Throughout that time we used to hear stories from our grandma and grandpa about the way our people used to live. They never sat down and told us our history like you would in the classroom. But they would mention and emphasize that something was important in our life, and we remembered those things. And after years and years you kind of collectively put these things together and start learning the history of our people.

Chief Weahwewa was my great, great grandfather. My grandpa was Sam Wewa. His dad was Charley Wewa, and Charley's dad was Chief Weahwewa. Charley Wewa was an

Indian doctor. He knew about plants, and he used to pray for people to make them well. He did it the way our old people used to. He also had songs for healing people. And he had ways that he talked to people to make their life get better.

Chief Weahwewa was a leading chief among all the Northern Paiutes in Oregon, Idaho, and perhaps northern Nevada. Everybody knew him, and that's why our family was well known in my day, because of him. All of the old people I talked with and all of the reservations I visited knew about Weahwewa. That's why they knew of our family. And that's why, even today, many people still have a lot of respect for the Wewa family, because of that connection to Chief Weahwewa.

Chief Weahwewa was the older brother of Chief Paulina. My grandpa Sam Wewa wasn't an Indian doctor, but Sam's older brother, Frank, was an Indian doctor. I think that a lot of our knowledge gets passed on by the spiritual people of our tribes, because they know the things that are secret and the things they can share. I think that's why our family knew quite a bit about our history, about our legends and about the plants, and especially about the medicines. These things were passed down to me.

I also learned a lot of family history while traveling. When I was a little boy we once stayed with an old couple in Alturas, California. His name was George Brown, and he was our relative. George remembered Paul Paulina, the son of Chief Paulina. I learned about the other part of our family, the Paulina family, from George Brown. And that's when I learned about Paul Paulina. He was an Indian doctor. He used to practice at Fort Bidwell and Beatty and on the Pyramid Lake Reservation. People would call on Paul requesting him to pray for them and sing his songs to heal them of their sicknesses. My dad once took me over where he thought Paul Paulina was buried. I always remember where our relatives are buried out there. I heard stories about that from my dad.

There was an old lady from Burns named Marion Louie. When we would go down to Burns to dig roots, my grandma and I and Marion Louie used to talk about Weahwewa. Because she spoke broken English, Marion Louie talked to my grandma in Paiute. So it was hard for me to understand her. But she spoke good Paiute. My grandma would talk to her about Weahwewa. One time we learned that Marion Louie knew where Weahwewa was buried—at the base of Steens Mountain. She said that we would need a four-wheel drive pickup to go there. "We should go there sometime," she told my grandma, "to visit the burial place." We never went.

### Travels with My Grandmother, Learning Legends from the Elders

Our people often live in the areas they had traditionally traveled through. We heard that from our grandma and grandpa, and from my uncle, my aunt, and my dad. They used to tell us all kinds of stories. As I said, they never really sat down and talked to us about our history and legends. But as I got older my grandma used to tell me stories when we were traveling.

When I graduated from high school, not too long after the loss of our grandpa, I got a car from my parents. I enjoyed that car and so did my grandma. I think my grandma was having a hard time dealing with the loss of our grandpa. Through the stories she used to tell, she would talk about all those places that she used to go when she was young. She would tell us about the time she received a letter from Owyhee, Nevada, which is over by Elko, Nevada. Our relatives there wrote a letter to my grandma and said that they were going to have a *peyote* meeting at Owyhee, on whatever the date was. So my grandma had one of her in-laws, a lady named Montola, ride with her from Warm Springs *clear* over to there to Owyhee on horseback. It takes about ten hours, going between fifty and seventy miles an hour, to get over there now. But way back in the early 1900s they went on horseback! So when she got to go to those places my grandma would tell about the people she knew and met, and about our relatives and extended family.

When Grandma told me what she used to do it made me interested to see where she went. So after I got the car that year I called Grandma and said, "Do you want to go to Owyhee? We'll go down there and see if any of the people you knew are still alive, and see our other relatives. We'll go down and see them." She said, "Sure, let's go."

So we made plans to go down there during the Fourth of July. That was the start of my real learning from my grandma. When we went, she started reminiscing about all the old people that she knew. She started thinking, "Well, this person is probably gone now, because they were already old when we were down there before." She didn't know who would still be there. Then she thought, "Well, all of my nieces and nephews from our relatives down there were little kids when we went before." She said, "They are probably the same age as your dad now. Maybe they don't remember who I am."

We went there for the Fourth of July. They used to have a *big* Fourth of July down there. They had our traditional stick game. And they had round dances and a rodeo and a big encampment. Our people had wall tents they would put up. It had a kitchen and everything. And they would put up shades made out of willows. They've got a lot of willows down there in Duck Valley. So they shaded the front of the wall tent with the willows. *Everybody* went to the Fourth of July grounds.

I had an aunt over there. Her name was Eva Been. So when we got there we went to look for her and found her. When the older people saw my grandma, they started coming over. They would ask her if she was Maggie Wewa, and she said, "Yes." Then they started talking to her in Paiute. More and more people came over to see her throughout the time we were there, about four days. A lot of people came and sat and talked with my grandma and my aunt. My aunt had a food stand and was selling coffee and stuff like that. So my grandma just sat right there in her chair and people came and sat by her and visited with her. Up until that point I had never heard my Grandma talk Indian, talk the Paiute language. She always talked English. I think she did that because a lot of the old people in Warm Springs that talked our language were dying, so there was hardly anybody left for her to talk to.

When my dad and others went to boarding school, they didn't allow them to talk Indian. They would get into trouble for talking their own language. Their mouths would be washed out with brown bar soap if they spoke Paiute. Or they would have to do chores, like washing the tile floors on their hands and knees with a little bitty, tiny brush, about the size of a toothbrush. They got punished for talking their own language. When we grew up we never heard them talk Indian very much. I didn't hear my dad talk Paiute to my mom, because my mom wasn't Paiute. She was Palouse and Walla Walla from the Umatilla Reservation. They never talked to one another in Indian, because those two languages, Paiute and Palouse, aren't related to each other. So we grew up learning English.

On that weekend in Owyhee we met a lot of our people and heard a lot of Paiute. Then one of my aunts took us home. She said we should go home with her because one of my other grandmas was there, and she and my grandma wanted to visit. We went home with them so they could catch up and talk Paiute. Hearing them talk, I could not understand what was being said. So when we came home from down there I asked my grandma, "What were you guys talking about when you were talking to Lillie?" Grandma responded, "She's telling me about the people I used to know, which ones are still alive, which ones died, and all that kind of stuff. She was glad to see me." So they just caught up on probably thirty or forty years of news. And I got to know my relatives and elders down there in Owyhee.

Then Fort Hall, over by Pocatello, Idaho, had a big celebration. I told Grandma, "Fort Hall's coming up in August. Do you want to go to Fort Hall?" She said, "Yeh, we'll go." And she started saving money. Then my cousin Rosie decided to go with us. Three of us went. Because I didn't know how far it was, we needed another driver, and she went. When we were traveling to Fort Hall, that's when we heard the stories Grandma used to tell us. We used to come first to Bend and then drive across to Burns and Ontario, and on east to Fort Hall. At that time there was a two-lane highway.

So, that's one of the times when Grandma would tell us stories, when we were getting over on the other side of Burns. It was at a place they call Drewsey, up in the middle of the desert. It wasn't on the highway, but there was an old gas pump there, one of those old red ones you used to pump by hand. She said, "This is where our people used to live. All this land is where our people used to stay, where Juntura is."

My grandma told me that the 1878 war started around Fort Hall and around Drewsey. I don't think she was specifically saying that it started at Drewsey. My grandma used to talk about general areas, and so Burns and Drewsey and all that area over there—this is where the war started. I asked her, "Which war?" She told us about the time the Bannocks came from Idaho to Boise and got into a fight with the white people there. This happened because the ranchers and farmers were starting to put up fences on Indian land all along the Boise valley, and all along the rivers. And they didn't want the Paiutes cutting down their fences and going across *their* land, they said. So the Bannocks complained to the army at Fort Boise, but they wouldn't do anything about it. The war started because, when the Bannocks went out to one of the places they used to dig camas called Camas Prairie, there was a whole bunch of pigs in there! And the pigs were digging up all the camas bulbs and eating them! So the Bannocks killed all the pigs, and the farmer or rancher got mad. He tried to tell them something, and then words were exchanged and shots were fired. That's when the war started.

We went on to Fort Hall. Aunt Eva lived in Fort Hall. She had a house in Owyhee, and that's why she would go down to Owyhee on the Fourth of July. We went to Fort Hall to find her sitting at a food stand there. That was a way she made money. When we went to her house she said, "You guys, come eat at the Senior Citizens Community Center," because she used to cook there.

So one day we went down there to eat. When we walked in a lot of the people, mostly old ladies, knew my grandma. They came up and asked her, "Are you Maggie Wewa?" And then they talked to her in Paiute. They were glad to see her. There were some that still remembered her. So we sat at the table with them and they talked Paiute. It did no good to try to listen, because my cousin and I didn't understand Paiute. So we just talked with our hands and talked among ourselves.

Then my grandma told us, "This is your relative. Her name was Nora Teton." She was related to my grandpa, Sam Wewa. She had a sister named Lucy Teton, who had died previously. They were my grandpa's relatives. My grandma had a pair of moccasins that Lucy had made for her back in the 1920s, when she gave them to my grandma. Nora remembered those moccasins and asked if she still had them? Grandma told her, "Yeh, I got them." I asked her, "What kind?" She said, "Oh, they're cut bead moccasins." So I asked, "How come you don't wear them?" And this got our interest. So one day after we came back from Fort Hall we asked Grandma, "Show us those moccasins that Lucy bead worked for you." So she dug them out of her trunk and showed them to us. They were really, really beautiful floral design, cut bead moccasins.

So Grandma told us how my grandpa, Sam Wewa, was related to the Tetons of Fort Hall. My grandma was related to the Edmo family of Fort Hall. So that is how we knew we had relatives there.

We also have relatives at Owyhee, Fort McDermitt, Summit Lake, Fort Bidwell, and on the Klamath Reservation. That was because when the Paiute and Bannock war of 1878 ended, our people were disbanded, split up, and went back to live in some of their own traditional areas. And they went to live with relatives in other areas. So our family got split up that way, too. But through the years from that time on until the 1970s, our people still remembered our family ties. And we met a lot of older people who were our relatives.

So while traveling with my grandma from 1970 clear up until when she passed away in 1987, she told us a *lot* of stories. And she introduced us to a lot of people. Wherever we went we never had to stay in a motel. That was because a lot of people knew my grandma, and they knew my grandpa, and they knew our family. So we got invited to stay in their homes, the old way. People wanted you to stay in their home and to take care of you. All their kids would sleep on the floor, and all of us visitors would get the beds. That's how they took care of us, and cooked for us. And we had a place to shower and clean up.

We used to live at a lot of different homes when we traveled to different places to go to a funeral. After I had a car somebody would call and say that somebody had died in Beatty. Grandma would say, "That's our relative, so we would go." So she and I, and maybe my cousin Francis, or maybe my cousin Rosie, we would go to the funeral. At the funeral people would see my grandma. It was at funerals, too, that we met more people and they would tell us that they were our relatives.

We also traveled to dig roots. When we traveled, like to the Beatty area, somebody would tell us, "Well, you should come down in June and dig *yapa*." That is one of the roots my people used to dig. My Grandma would say that the Paiute people from that area were called *Yapatikadu*, or "Indian carrot eaters." That's how she would tell us things like that. She never elaborated, but she would just say, "They called these people *Yapatikadu*. They dig *yapa* here." Over years of putting these things together I got to know where our people lived in those days.

So from the seventies on, when I started taking my grandma around, I met a lot of old people and we would sit and talk. I think it was important to them to remember the old days. So they would talk about the Bannock and Paiute Wars. And they would talk about the wars the Paiutes had against the soldiers in Oregon. They would talk about how they were related to us. And they would talk about people that were significant in their families. They might have been a chief or a leader or a good hunter or an Indian doctor, but they were well remembered. I heard a lot of those stories when traveling with my grandma.

When I was about five years old my grandma and grandpa would load my cousins and me in the pickup to go with them and dig roots. We would go to Burns in the springtime, around the end of April or May, because that's when the roots would come out. So my cousins and I would end up seeing each other then. Our people used to dig *kangedya*, they called it bitter-root, and *tsuga*, desert parsley. So we would travel with my grandma and grandpa to go to Burns to dig roots. Sometimes my grandpa would take us in his pickup and drop us all off over there. I don't know how long we would stay, maybe a week or maybe two weeks. But we would stay over in the Burns area during the root season.

I went with them a couple of times in the springtime. The first time our grandpa took us in his pickup, and the second time my grandma and I went on the bus. We caught the bus at Madras and rode to Bend and then east into the desert. At that time the pavement ended at Millican, and from there on it was a dirt road, clear to 395, over by Riley. It was a long trip.

When we rode the bus over that way it stopped at Hampton. It used to be almost an all-day trip to go from Madras to Burns, so we would stop at Hampton to eat lunch. When we'd stop at Hampton, all of the white people would get off the bus and go to eat in the café there. But my grandma and I did something different. She used to make a quilt cover out of denim pants. She would take the old denim pants from my dad or my uncles and cut them up and sew them together to make a quilt cover. And she would use that denim quilt cover to put on the ground to sit on when they'd go someplace.

So in Hampton we went around to the shady side of the building and put my grandma's denim quilt cover down, and then sat down on the ground to eat. She would have a big jar of water, those canning jars with water in it. And she would have a paper bag with homemade biscuits, fried deer meat, some roots from the previous year, and maybe pastry. We'd sit on that denim quilt cover outside the restaurant, on the side of the building in the shade, and eat. It wasn't because the white people didn't want us in there. It was just how my grandmother traveled.

Eventually she would say, "We better get on the bus now, we're going to go." So we'd put all of our stuff away, and we would go get on the bus and go to Burns. As I mentioned earlier, we never thought we were poor or rich. But we always had enough to eat, and sometimes I felt a lot richer than a lot of people.

Our relatives in Burns used to live up on a hill, and you could see their houses from the road. I don't know how she could tell, but when my grandma would look up there she would say, "There's nobody home up there. They must be all at the root camp." So we'd go to the bus depot in Burns, and she'd pay the bus driver a couple of dollars to take us out into the desert. We were going to Stinking Water Pass, I think they called it. I remember one time when we got up there she argued with the bus driver, "Drop us off anywhere along here." "No," he said, "There's nothing and nobody out here." But she said, "This is where we're going to get off." He didn't want to drop us off out there in the middle of nowhere, but she finally talked him into it. So he stopped the bus in the road and we got off.

When we got off in the desert I had a little bitty tin blue suitcase, and she got off with her bundle. She had a bundle tied up with blankets, and inside of it our bedding and stuff, and her clothes. Then we stashed our stuff under a juniper tree off the road and walked out into the desert. We found our people camped out there, digging roots. I had an uncle camped out with them. His name was Doyle Charles, and he had a pickup.

I had to go back to the highway with him and get our stuff from under the juniper tree, and get it loaded on the truck and come back to the root camp.

That's when I heard even more stories and legends. There was an old man out there and his name was Davey Jim. He was an older Paiute man. He used to stay at the camp when others went out digging. Or he would go gather dried juniper limbs for the fires. We didn't have Coleman stoves then, so they cooked over an open fire. The old ladies did the cooking. So when our people came in with roots, some of them would sit down on their blankets and peel the roots.

And sometimes toward evening that old man, Davey Jim, would tell us stories. There were other kids out there in the desert. I don't remember who they were, but they were Paiute kids, too. So he would tell us all stories. And sometimes, when the old ladies were gone or away, he would tell us colorful Coyote stories—the ones that were kind of X-rated. The old ladies didn't like him telling us that kind of stuff. But when I would go to get water with him or my Uncle Doyle I learned some of those stories from them.

We used to go get water in tin milk cans. We'd get spring water in those tin milk cans. When we went with them to get water Davey Jim would point out things and tell us the Paiute name for them. We might see frogs and lizards or water snakes or dogs at the stream, and he would tell us the Paiute name for them.

My grandpa also taught me the names of juniper, sagebrush, lizard, deer, and antelope, and plant names. He also showed me a medicine for toothache. When we were down there in the desert digging roots there was a little girl with an earache. So they got some kind of plant medicine and warmed it and made it like tea. Then they dropped it in her ear. I don't know what it was but it seemed to help her. They also used to blow smoke in the ear as a form of medicine. So the next day that old man, Davey Jim, got a cigarette and smoked it and blew smoke in her ear. That helped her get rid of the pain and made her earache go away. I saw those kinds of things when I was little, and down there in the desert digging roots with my grandma and grandpa.

There's a place called Castle Rock that you could see from where we used to dig roots. The Paiute called that *Tukwahane*. It was a sacred place for the Paiutes. The first time it was ever brought to my attention was during a big spring thunderstorm, when people were getting ready for the storm. They would say, "Oh, the wind is going to start blowing!" Then everybody would start anchoring everything down. And just like that a big wind would come up, "whooooo," and blow through the camp, knocking over buckets and all kinds of stuff. Then it would start raining, and there were big thunder clouds over Castle Rock. It seemed like the lightening was just drawn to that hill—BOOM!!! CRASH!!!—just drawn to that one spot. You could see the lightning hit Castle Rock.

That's when the people talked to us about *Tukwahane*. They said that's where our past people used to go, a long time ago, to get power. They would go up there and stay and get power, for that is a very sacred place for our people.

Our grandpa took us down there one other time. On that trip we stayed in the back of the pickup with the tailgate down, and slept with our heads toward the tailgate. I'd be in between my grandma and grandpa. That's when my grandpa would show me the stars and ask me, "Can you see that deer?" At that time I didn't know what he was talking about. He explained that it was like connecting the dots, with a line going from dot to dot. And he would show me one thing at a time, saying: "There's the head, there's the legs, and there's the tail." "See the hummingbird?" And he'd show me a little group of stars and say, "That's its nose," probably meaning its beak, "and that's its body." So he showed me the stars and the animals in our constellations. We had names for the constellations, too.

I learned about the stars from my grandpa. He told me, and my dad later told me, that we know when it's time to go hunting because the constellation with the deer moves from one position to another. So when it gets to be hunting time we can look up into the stars and the sky and know it's time to go hunting. So, our people knew about watching the stars to do certain things.

I think a lot of times the anthropologists that study our people think our people didn't know things like that. Our people knew a lot of things because we knew about everyday life and nature. When the anthropologists came there were things that our people didn't think were significant or appropriate to share with them.

Going back to my family history, Weahwewa was recognized as a chief of all the Northern Paiute people. When the white people and the soldiers first came to this country, our people used to live all over Central Oregon. I know that because of the legends and the names of geographic features in Central Oregon. Mostly I know Central Oregon because that's where I grew up. And when my grandma was alive, we traveled all around Central Oregon. This land, clear from the Warm Springs area, clear across to the Burns area, clear down to Silver Lake, was pretty much recognized as Weahwewa's territory and Paulina's territory. That's where their camps were. That's where their food was. And that's where our people gathered their food and lived.

Our people told us this story as part of our oral history. Our people said that some of the covered wagons came through the mountains east of Prineville, somewhere over there, and the people in those wagons were pitiful. They were starving, so the Paiutes tried to take them deer meat and tried to take them roots. But when the Paiutes would start going toward them, the emigrants would fire guns at them. So the Paiutes backed off and left them alone. Then they'd see the emigrants burying their dead along the trail. The Indians couldn't figure out why they wouldn't eat anything. They'd make fires at night, but they wouldn't eat, so their people were sick and dying. The Paiute elders at Burns used to say, "They were dying and there were all kinds of chokecherries growing all around them, next to the creek. But they weren't eating them. And there were a lot of roots on the hillsides. But they wouldn't eat them either. That's why they died, because they didn't know how to live out here. And when our people tried to help them they shot at us."

I recently listened to an audio tape of an old lady, Marion Louie. I guess she was preserving some of her stories, like I'm doing now. She talked about wagons coming into the Harney Valley country. There were Paiute girls playing as those wagons were coming down the hill, and the girls made up a song. I can't sing the song because I don't know it well enough. But the song was saying that there were people coming through the dust. Because all of those wagons were making a lot of dust, and all they could see was the oxen pulling the wagons, coming out of the dust. They made a Paiute song about those people.

Then they ran and told our people about the white people coming out of the dust. And this time the emigrants allowed the Paiutes to help them. So our people fed them deer meat and roots, and helped them get back on their journey. Then they went on to wherever they were going, west of the mountains. And because of that they survived. After that, and after they helped those white people, the Paiute girls made their song about those people coming out of the dust.

Pretty soon our people were having to compete with miners and settlers for food. They were killing all the deer, and the antelope, and their cattle were chomping up and destroying all the root digging grounds we relied on for food. So our people looked at the cattle as food. To them it was just like making a trade: "You guys are doing this to our food, so we're going to take the cattle as trade for our food." And that was a way of life.

That's when the Warm Springs people signed up with the army to become scouts for the military. And while they were scouts for the military the Warm Springs Indians were issued guns by the military. That made them all believe they were fierce warriors. I don't think they were ever warriors before that time. But when they got guns and horses they became warriors. Then they led the soldiers to places the Paiutes would be camping, or where they used to be, like Prineville.

Prineville used to be a Paiute village, a wintering village up that canyon toward the reservoir. There were a lot of willows that grew along that part of the Crooked River and our people used willows and pine pitch to make water bottles and baskets. They used those willows for making all kinds of things they needed to store food. There were other villages along Crooked River. Over by the bridge east of Smith Rock, the bridge that comes out at Grizzly Mountain, there was a village there, too. My grandma told me that there were villages over there. She said there were villages all along the Crooked River. So that must have been an awfully good place to winter and find food.

Because there were lots of roots that our people dig around there, all around Prineville and all around Smith Rock.

Going back to my family, Paulina was the youngest brother. In their younger days, Paulina and Weahwewa were always together, warring against the whites in Central Oregon. A lot of fences were being put up by the big cattle owners, like Howard Maupin and Peter French. They were fencing off portions of the land. Some of the other big cattle ranchers in Central Oregon were making fences too. But the Paiute people didn't know what fences were for. So when they came up to a fence they'd pull it down. Then they could pass through, just like they had for thousands of years, and not be impeded by any kind of a structure as they moved across the land.

The ranchers got tired of the Indians doing that. So they would fire on defenseless villages of mostly women and children and old people and kill them. When the Paiute men would return to their village that was burned and sacked and ravaged by the white people, they would retaliate by raiding the white settlements, the miners in Canyon City, John Day area, and all those little mining towns. They would raid them. The white people believed that the Indians were making war on them. So they went up to the Oregon Territorial government asking for help.

The white people called it a war. But the Paiutes didn't think there was a war. They were only protecting what was theirs. These days we get to put terms on things that people do. And if I look back I would say that my great-grandfathers Weahwewa and Paulina, as well as the leaders Oytes and Watah, and all those Paiute chiefs were patriots, just like Paul Revere, George Washington, and Thomas Jefferson. They were protecting their families, their land, their livelihood, and their way of life. Because invaders were coming, ranchers and farmers, and they were putting up things our people never understood—fences.

And they were saying that the land belonged to them, when our people had used it for thousands of years and tens of thousands of years. Our people used it to dig roots and hunt on and to live on, and to use the spring water as we chose. So to have the white people building homesteads and fencing off the springs, all of that was foreign to the Paiute people. So they would tear down the fences so they could continue to cross the land, as they always had. Then, inevitably, some Paiutes would get killed. So our men would retaliate. Maybe they were gone that day, and then when the men came back they would go and raid, not knowing whether it was this miner over here or that rancher over there that did it. They would just go raid to retaliate for their family being killed.

About that same time, in June of 1855, a treaty created the Warm Springs Reservation that now exists, and the Columbia River people were moved to it. This is when a lot of battles started, because we had not discussed or agreed to it, and because it was our land. Also, rather than having to go all the way to the Columbia River to raid those people, and finding corrals full of horses and cattle at Warm Springs, the Paiutes raided the agency on the Warm Springs Reservation. A couple of times the Paiutes drove the soldiers and agency workers and Indians all the way back to Fort Dalles! That went on until they got reinforcements and bigger numbers. Then they came back and retook Warm Springs. By then the Paiutes had driven off the cattle and horses, because for them that was food and transportation.

Then the military came, the army. I don't know whether it was the army, militia, volunteers, or whatever. Arguing over terms is white people stuff, it's not ours. But in the stories our grandparents told us it was the army, so I call it the army. To our people they were the army. They came to protect the settlers and the ranchers and the farmers, and to chase after the Paiutes.

Then after the wars the government created the Malheur Indian Reservation. When they were going to sign a treaty in 1872 to make the Malheur Indian Reservation, they called all the Paiute leaders together to discuss this treaty. There were ten Paiute leaders, ten main ones, that signed the treaty. There were probably more, but they didn't make it to the treaty council. There was a place down there by Burns called Fort Harney. That's where they were getting ready to sign the treaty. The army kept talking to the other Paiute leaders and telling them, "This is what we're going to do for your people." But one of them—I can't remember his name, said, "You'll have to wait till our father gets here." When I first heard about this I didn't know what they were talking about, so I asked my grandma, "Who was their dad?" She said, "No, they're talking about Weahwewa. They used to refer to the old leaders as our father, because they're just like a father of the people. They take care of everybody. So they had to wait for him to get there."

General Howard, I think it was, didn't want to wait. He wanted to hurry and negotiate and get it signed and get it done with, just like they had done with other tribes and treaties. But the Paiute leaders said, "We have to wait for Weahwewa to come. We have to wait for our father." So they held off a couple of days.

Finally somebody came riding into camp and said, "He's coming. He's coming now." Chief Louie was later the chief of the Burns Paiutes. But he was a young man at that time, and he was there at the time of the treaty. Chief Louie later told his daughter, Marion Louie, that Weahwewa was coming in, and that his hair was all white. Marion Louie told my grandma, "He still could ride a horse and his hair was white."

When Chief Weahwewa got there, they explained to the Paiute leaders what the treaty was going to be. They said that

Paiutes had to lay down their arms and quit warring against the white people. In exchange for stopping the war, the Paiutes would get the lands that they would choose for their reservation. The white people wouldn't be allowed to come on those lands or enter there. That would be their land forever. So they signed the treaty, and those old leaders took the negotiators and the surveyors and pointed out where they wanted the reservation to be. That became the boundary of the reservation. It went from the Strawberry Mountains in the north, to south of Canyon City, down toward Silvies Creek, clear down around the Steens Mountain, clear back across and up to the Strawberry Mountains. The tribal elders told everyone where they wanted their reservation to be and that was the boundary they agreed on. They wrote it down on the paper and it became part of the treaty.

It was through these discussions that we learned about my great-great grandfather, Weahwewa. We learned how important he was as a leader of the people. And how they used to call him him *Mu naa'a*, which means "our father," because he was such a leader. And when they made that treaty he hoped that our people would always have the land. It didn't work out that way, but that's what he wanted. Sometime after that, sometime after the treaty, Chief Weahwewa died.

It was in 1872 the United States government agreed to the treaty with the Paiute people forming the Malheur Reservation in southeast Oregon. It had 1.7 million acres and was the biggest reservation in Oregon. But because of the Bannock War in 1878 they never ratified that treaty into law. Because of the war the federal government didn't sign it.

The war was a result of the federal government not following through on the promises it made to the Paiute people in that treaty. They promised them a schoolhouse. They promised a mill. They promised houses. They were promised annuities or rations for a number of years, as long as the Paiutes stayed on the reservation and quit war with the white people. And they promised them that reservation. They never did follow through with fulfilling any of the promises they made to our people.

Soon after that the Paiutes went to different places, to Fort McDermit, Fort Bidwell, Beatty, and elsewhere. My people, the Wewas, the Johnsons, and some other families, were all sent to Fort Simcoe on the Yakima Reservation, and to Fort Vancouver. Then they ended up at Warm Springs.

Later my grandfather got involved in the work of the Indian Claims Commission. And my Grandpa Sam became involved in the fight to recover our lands and rights. My grandpa went to the meetings in Owyhee. He went to the meetings in Fort Hall. He went to the meetings at Beatty. And he went to the meetings at Burns. He was chosen as one of the representatives for the Paiutes. So they started making a list of all the descendants of the chiefs that signed that Malheur Treaty, and who their people were, and which chief the people fell under. My grandpa did that. There were others that did it too. But my grandpa was a key part of that compilation of this data. So they made a grievance to the Indian Claims Commission, which was a special investigative commission of the federal government. They would investigate wrongs that were done to different tribes in the United States, and the Paiutes made their grievance before that Indian Claims Commission.

When my grandpa died, he had a briefcase with all those documents in it. He had a lot of things from the Indian Claims Commission, and letters and testimony that came to him. My grandma had that briefcase for a while. Then my aunt took possession of it. Then, before my aunt died, she gave me that leather briefcase with all those papers in it. So I'm the keeper of all that now, of all those documents that prove what I know and what I am saying is true, because it is written down. A lot of white people don't believe us because what we have isn't written down. So I have those documents in my possession.

My Uncle Melvin, my dad's older brother, was on the tribal council. And he went on the trips to the hearings in Carson City. At another time my Aunt Christine was on the council, too. And she heard the stories. So they went down to the hearings — and this was when there were still old people alive that remembered the Malheur Reservation. They were the ones making testimony before the Indian Commission. Because they understood Paiute, my dad, my uncle, my aunt, and my grandma heard firsthand from people that were in their nineties at that time. They heard about the war in 1878, and about all the things that happened to our people after that time. These elders were giving testimony to the Indians Claim Commission at that time. So my dad, my aunt, and my uncle heard from people that lived through all of this firsthand, from people that lived that life.

They had fought against the soldiers, so they could talk some English. And they had several interpreters from the government. The government hired them to get accurate testimony when the elders were talking to the Indian Claims Commission in Paiute. My dad and my uncle heard these stories firsthand.

So my dad and my Uncle Melvin and my Aunt Chris would all go down to Carson City for the hearings of that commission. These hearings had almost all the Paiutes fired up and believing that something was finally being done. And everybody was recalling their family histories. That's when I got to know more about my dad's side of the family.

That's how I learned a lot of these stories and legends and this history. I learned where our people used to gather different kinds of roots and where they would hunt. I learned about battle places. And I learned about the places where we used to camp, where there was good grass, or where there were petroglyphs or pictographs. I learned about these things while traveling throughout those areas from the time I first got my car in 1975 until today.

When we would go to Beatty, we had some grandmas down there. One was named Judy Watah. And we had another grandma, and her name was Mattie Wewa. They were two old ladies that lived together down there. When we would stay there they would talk about old times, about our history and that kind of stuff. I used to hear them talk about those things with my dad.

They used to tell us stories and legend, too. I remember what they used to tell us, my brother Matt and me. I think that's where I learned the legend of Old Lady Frog. There used to be frogs by their spring. So she told us that legend, and I remembered it. My brother, Matt, is gone now. But I know the legend.

When I was a young teenager, and in my early twenties, I was already talking to the people and sharing stories. If I would say something wrong my family would correct me, saying, "You don't know what you're talking about!" Then they'd correct me on things I was saying when I would talk to the people. My family was real instrumental in my education and what I know about our people today.

As I traveled with my grandma and family I met more and more of our old people, the few old people that are still left today. I guess this made me think about myself. I hardly have any friends my own age. All my friends are old people. I enjoy sitting with old people and hearing their stories. A friend once said to me, "That's how you are. You're always sitting with the elders listening and talking, and sharing the stories of our people."

## What the Legends Meant to the Paiute People

The book that you're about to read is very important because historically many of the thoughts and perceptions of Native American people have been from the perspective of the non-native peoples. This experience is not particular to the United States or North America. Rather, it reflects a process that has been used around the world by anthropologists, historians, and explorers when they have come across native people they didn't understand. Many times their interpretations, and I emphasize *their*, have been wrong about native peoples. The present endeavor involves a sharing of my story, and reflects decades of compilation of history, legends, and lifeways, the gathering of traditional foods and medicines and the spiritual ways of the Northern Paiute people. This is the first time that I, Wilson Wewa, have told these legends, after having used the better part of my life listening to our elders and learning as much as I can from the elders who were living in my lifetime.

The gathering of stories and legends for this book is important because the technology that is being adopted by people around the world, particularly Native American children, has pushed oral traditions aside, in preference to using those technologies. Many times our young people have doubted the accuracy of oral stories, histories, and lifeways, in favor of what has been written by non-native professionals. So this work is being put together to record the thoughts and stories of our ancestors. These were transmitted in the traditional way, from one person to another, in hopes that my children, my grandchildren, and all the young people that follow long after I'm gone will look back and know that someone took the time and energy to save these stories and put this book together. I hope this will help instill and bring back the pride that our people had in their identity.

The histories and the lifeways of the Paiute people—and these legends—are all intertwined with their life in the Great Basin. It has often been said that legends are a corruption of historical events from the past, put into the amusing form to catch the interest of the listener. To me these legends are not only entertainment that was used to captivate a Northern Paiute audience, sitting around a small campfire in a cattail or willow mat shelter during the winter. Today they can also be used as an instrument of education, or as storytelling in a classroom or home, to once again help fill in the void felt by young people trying to understand their history and identity and searching for who they are.

Today there are many young people among the Northern Paiutes who are hungry for this type of nurturing and learning. Because of various restrictions, some of them I've known have not had the time, the money, the gas, or other resources needed to search out and find the elders who still carry these stories and this knowledge in their heads. And this search can be very time-consuming. Some forty years of traveling for recreation, for sightseeing, and for reconnecting with long-forgotten relatives and friends have helped me gather the legends I am now trying to communicate.

I hope that one day these stories can be used to help spell out geographical areas, building sites, mountains, rivers, canyons, food-gathering areas, hunting sites of our people. And I hope that one day these stories will once again show that the Oregon desert and the Great Basin were not as inhospitable and bleak as many people now make them out to be. For these stories show that when the Northern Paiute people roamed the vast extent of this land they were able to make a living using all of the resources that the Creator left here on this earth for us as gifts.

It is also my hope that my people never forget those resources. In my heart—and I'll truly believe this till the day I die—the Paiute people have never, ever given up our land and its resources in the Great Basin. We have been forced to change, but they can never take the Indian out of our heart. And as long as we keep alive the Indian within ourselves, we'll always be a part of that Paiute heritage. And part of being a Northern Paiute, a little part of it, has now been told and written in the legends and stories of this book.

I encourage all readers, young and old, to close your eyes and allow yourself to drift back into the past, as you get ready to read these legends. In that way, through the dreams and stories of our people, you'll more fully understand our people and this work.

# Legends of the Northern Paiute

## LEGEND 1

# The Creation Story and the Malheur Cave

In our legends the world began at the base of Steens Mountain. That is where Coyote and Wolf created the world we have today. Wolf was called *Mu naa'a*, our father, because he was the father of all of creation.

At the time there was nothing in the world. It was just dark. But our people could hear one another in the darkness, and they talked about making a world.

Wolf told Coyote to go out from the darkness and find land. Coyote went out, but he could not find anyplace. So they asked, "Who would dive under the water?"

Different animals in the darkness volunteered to dive into the water. The first one was Otter. He said, "I'm a good swimmer. I will go and see what is holding up the water." Then the Otter swam down for one day and then two days, before he came back up. He had almost drowned! He said he couldn't find anything down under the water. He never even made it to the bottom.

Then Muskrat said, "I'll go next." He said, "I am a good swimmer, better than Otter." He dove into the water and went

3

down, and down, and down. . . . He was gone for one day, and then two days. On the third day he came back up. He was *sooo* tired, and he was starving! But he said that he never made it to the bottom of the water either.

The third one who said, "Let me try" was the Mud Hen, *Saya*. Mud Hen said, "I'll go down and see what is holding up the water." Mud Hens are real small little birds. Everyone asked, "You want to go?" But Wolf said, "Go ahead and try." So Mud Hen dove into the water and went *waaay* down there. When it came back up it had mud on the end of its bill, and there was some grass on that mud! Wolf and the Coyote stood on that piece of mud.

Then Coyote said, "I'm getting tired of standing here all the time. This land needs to get bigger." Wolf, his older brother, started singing his song, a doctor song. While he was singing, the land started getting bigger and bigger and bigger. When he would stop singing, Wolf and Coyote would walk around on the land. But Coyote was always complaining, "This land should be bigger than this, so there will be room for both of us." So Wolf started singing again, and the land got bigger and bigger, and bigger and bigger.

This time Coyote walked to edge of the land to the east, to see how far the water was. When he came back he said, "Well, if we're going to put other people here, then this land has got to be bigger." He was talking about the animal people, not people like us human beings.

So Wolf sang his song again, and the land kept growing. For five days Wolf sang. When he finished, Coyote went off to find the edge of the land. He found the land had been made like it is today. When Coyote came back Wolf saw him coming and said, "Don't tell me this land isn't big enough now. That's all I'm going to do!"

That's how the world was created, half water and half land. After the world was made the Fish in the water started swimming into the land. And when they swam into the land they made the creeks and the rivers. It was their tails moving back and forth that made the water go up into the land. Then Wolf told the Fish, "That's where you're going to be now! You'll always be in the water."

When the Coyote left again to go to the east, the Fish there were swimming into the dirt, too. They were making rivers over there on the other side, in the eastern part of the world. That's how the rivers were created by the Fish that came in from the oceans.

At the time the world was made there was darkness, and the other animals were still in the darkness. They said, "I think Wolf, *Mu naa'a,* has made a world now. We should go there." They were wandering around in darkness, and one of the voices said, "Grab onto my tail." And they started going. All the animals were holding onto each other's tails, following one another in the darkness and out of the darkness.

When they were going they could see a light, as if you blocked out all the stars in the sky and left only one. They could see that light, and they started going that way. They traveled for five days, following one another. The one in front would sing, and they'd all go toward that light. And that light was getting bigger and bigger and bigger. Soon they came to the edge of the darkness, where that light was. And when they came out of that place up onto the dry ground, the place our people came out of was called Malheur Cave.

Bald Eagle was the first one that led them out of there. When he stuck his head out of the ground to see what was outside of the darkness, they let go of his tail. When he turned around to tell them what he saw up there, his tail went out—and then the light made his tail turn white, too. When he came out on the ground all the animals came out, and they saw this land as it is today. That's how the world was created and the animals came onto the land.

Then the animals went in all directions, north and south and all over. At that time the land was still wet and muddy, and nothing was growing on it.

Again, Coyote complained that there was no dry land to stand on. Wolf told the people to build fires at the edge of the water. So the animal people made fires to dry the land. Soon the land became dry. The birds flew over the earth, and dropped the seeds they found somewhere. These seeds made the grass and the trees grow.

After the earth was dry Wolf called them all together once again. He told them, "Now that you've all come on to this land, everybody has to pick where they're going to live."

That's when Bighorn Sheep, *Koepa*, said, "We're going to live in the mountains. We want to be in the rocks." So they moved into the mountains and they became *Koepa*. They said, "we like that name, *Koepa*," so that's what they became.

Deer said, "We like the mountains, too. But we don't want to be *way* up high. We want to be down where there's trees, and we want to be *Tuhudya*." So they became Deer, the Mule Deer.

Then all the animals said where they were going to live, and what they were going to be. And they all started naming themselves. So that's how they all named themselves.

Wolf was the leader, *moohedu*. That's why he was the one that was asking them, "Who do you want to be?" The next one said, "I'm going to be a Squirrel, and I'm going to make my home in the ground. So they became ground squirrels. It was the same with the groundhog. He wanted to live in the ground, too, but under the rocks. He chose the name *Kedu*.

At this time the animal people could all talk the same language. Then they started to argue with one another, and the animals that got along together moved to the same place and lived together. One day Wolf said, "I'm going to have a big meeting. I want everybody to come. You all put on your good clothes and come. I'm going to have a *big* meeting."

After Wolf's announcement, all the animals went to the mountains and found different colored rocks. They ground the rocks into paint. They got yellow paint and red paint, and blue and green and black and white paint. And they painted themselves! They wanted to be impressive to one another, and each one wanted to look better than the others. When they got to the meeting, Wolf looked at them and said, "What have you done to yourselves?" They were all painted up!

Then Wolf commanded, "From this day forward you're not going to talk to one another anymore, because you argue too much." So he changed them all into different kinds of animals. He made it so the Mountain Sheep couldn't talk to the Deer any more, and the Deer couldn't talk to the Birds, and the Birds couldn't talk to the Fish. And they could no longer make children together. Only Fish could be with Fish, only Eagles could be with other Eagles, and only Deer could be with other Deer. That's how they were all separated from each other. They could not talk a common language after that.

Today, the animals are still painted with the colors that they put on that day when they came to Wolf's meeting.

So that's how the animal people all came onto this land. In all the legends we never refer to them as animals. We always refer to them as people, because they were here first. They were the *Nuwuddu*. They were the first people. That is why we have this name, to respect them. And today we Paiutes call ourselves *Nuwu*, because we're the second people. It's the same word, but *Nuwuddu* is for the animal people, and *Nuwu* is for us, because we were created after the animal people.

That's how we were created. That's why Paiutes and animals are brothers and sisters. We're all the same.

# The Creation of the Human People

The animals created the Paiute people. There was some kind of a bird; it was a woman and she used to make baskets. The woman was an Oriole, because Orioles make basket nests. And Coyote, being how he was, used to be nasty. He wanted her because she used to make baskets and everything, and she was very pretty! But she didn't want to be with him. He wanted to be with her, but she kept pushing him away. She didn't want to be with him because he had a *bad* reputation.

Finally, Coyote talked her into going with him someplace. They were going along and they had a basket. It was a water bottle made out of willows and covered with pine pitch to keep it water tight. It is called *paosa*. As they were going along, he kept hearing a noise coming from that water bottle. Coyote told her, "Sounds like there's noise coming from inside that bottle." "Well, don't open it," she scolded him. "Leave it alone!" Then they kept going, and he got thirsty. He said, "I'm thirsty!" She told him, "Well, go down by the creek and get a drink." Coyote angrily said, "Well, there's a water bottle here, you should give me a drink." She replied, "No! Don't open that bottle!" Then the sun went down and they found a place to rest for the night.

The next day Coyote once again said, "Sound like there's people talking; a noise is coming from that bottle." The Oriole Woman kept telling him, "Don't open that bottle!" They continued to go along and the sun got kind of hot, and they took a rest underneath a big juniper tree. She lay down to take a nap, and set the bottle down beside her. But the bottle rolled away from her—and it started making noises again! Coyote was talking to her, but she wouldn't answer. Instead, she started to snore. Then Coyote knew she was asleep. So he snuck over by her side and got the bottle!

Sneakily, he pulled the plug out of the bottle. When he pulled the plug out—there were little people inside! They came out and started running off. Coyote tried to catch them and put them back in the bottle. But they were too fast for him. Some went south and some went east and west and north. And they were all different sizes. Some were kind of tall, and some were dark, and some were short. Some of them were light skinned and some were darker.

After they all ran away, Coyote once again looked inside the bottle. There was one boy and one girl left. So he turned the bottle upside down and shook it around. But they wouldn't come out of that bottle, so he reached in and pulled them out. They were kind of short, and they were the first two human people in this world. A man and a woman. That's why the Paiute people are short, because of what Coyote did. That's how the people were created.

# The Bridge of the Gods, the Great Floods, and the Human People

Most of the animal people were killed when the first great flood happened. Then the water went down, and that's when the human people got started.

In the time of the human people there was a second great flood that killed a lot of the human people, too. At some point, Mount St. Helens and Mount Hood erupted and blocked the Columbia River with lava. Then the water in the river backed up and flooded the low land all over the place—clear into the northern part of the Great Basin. It flooded all of that area, when that lava dam formed between Mount St. Helens and Mount Hood. Then, the river broke through and underneath that dam, and made the Bridge of the Gods, and the water started flowing again. That's when the water went down the first time.

Then our legends tell of a second great flood. At the time there was a big glacier in the Rocky Mountains. When it melted and receded it caused Montana and Wyoming and part of Canada to be underwater. When that glacier receded the water flooded through again. That second flood was in the time of the human people. That's when our people say that the Snake River flowed backward because the Bridge of the Gods was too narrow for all the water to come through. So it backed up and pushed up the canyons and made the Snake River flow backward.

That second flood destroyed the human people along the rivers and in low places, and our legends explain that.

## LEGEND 4

# How the Seasons Came to Be

A *looong* time ago all the animals were called together by
Wolf. Wolf was the leader. They all came together to discuss
the weather. All the animals that had long fur wanted it to be
cold all the time. But the animals that had no fur didn't want
it to be cold. At the time they were overpowered by the bigger
animals, so it was cool most of the time.

So Wolf called a big meeting and all the animals got together.
They never invited Coyote, because he was always a know-it-
all. He would say, "Oh, I was going to say that," or "I was
going to tell you guys we should do that." So they just didn't
invite him.

When they were at the meeting Wolf told them, "Well, we're
going to talk about whether it's good to have cool weather all
the time, or whether we're going to let it be warm."

First, Grizzly Bear stood up and said, "Well, I think it should
be cold all the time, because I have long fur, and I like to fish
in the water. When the water is cold there are a lot of Fish in
the water. But when it is warm the Fish go to the bottom of the
river, and it's hard to catch them. So I think the weather should
be cool all the time."

Others argued, "No, we don't want it like that!" And they argued back and forth.

Then Wolf told them, "Okay, let's be quiet. I want to hear from the Lizards."

So the spokesman for the Lizards said, "We don't want it to be cold all the time, because we can't come out of our home when it's cold all the time. We can't even come out to look around the land, because it's so cold we'd freeze. So we don't want it to be cold. And there are others like us that don't want it to be cold either."

Then they started arguing again. All the furry animals and all the ones with short hair were arguing about the cold.

While they were meeting, Coyote was wondering where all the people were. He asked, "Where did all the people go?" And he looked around saying, "I don't know where they went. It's quiet here, outside the house." So Coyote got up and looked around, and walked around the village. But the people had gone around the hill. They were meeting on the other side of the hill. When he came over the top of the hill he saw them all down there.

So he went there and asked, "What are you guys doing?"

Finally, Wolf told him, "Well, we're deciding on whether the weather should be cold all the time, or whether it should be warm. These folks over here want it to be cold all the time. And these folks over here want it to be warm." Then Wolf said, "Well, I think maybe we should have it cold half of the time and warm half of the time."

They responded, "*Nooo*. We don't want it like that!" Then they argued about it more. The weather would start an argument every time.

As Wolf was sitting there, Coyote started to get bossy, and said, "Well, I think it should be the way I said. You guys want it to be cold all the time. And you want warm all the time. But I think it should be the way *I* said it should be. Because the sun comes in the daytime and it warms everything up. In the nighttime the moon comes up, and everything cools down. And that's half the time. So, I think that's the way it should be."

Everybody was getting annoyed at Coyote for being so bossy. Then, as Wolf was standing there, one of the animals said, "Well, we should do what we never did. We should have a smoke." Because in the old days, before meetings started they use to smoke together.

But nobody had their pipe and tobacco. So one of the animals, Rabbit, said, "Coyote has a pretty pipe! He has the best pipe in the *whole* village!"

Coyote was looking at him and nodding his head in agreement, "Yeah!" Rabbit continued, "And he has good tobacco too! He makes *real* good tobacco. I think we should have Coyote bring his pipe, and then we'll smoke about this, while we're thinking how it's going to be."

Coyote put his chest out and was feeling *really* big, because the people were building him up. So Wolf looked at him and said, "Well, I guess we're going to smoke on this." Then Wolf said, "Coyote, my little brother, why don't you go back to your house and get your pipe?" They told him, "You have the best pipe. You should go get your pipe!" So Coyote got all built up as everybody said, "Yeah, yeah! Coyote, you should go get your pipe!"

So Coyote took off and went back around the hill, and back to his house. But he wasn't a good housekeeper. He was looking *all* over in there, and taking a long time looking for his pipe.

While he was gone the animals started talking again. They thought about Wolf's words, about half of the time being warm and half of the time being cold. Pretty soon they said, "No, it shouldn't be six months cold and six months warm. I think it should be three months cold and three months warm."

Then someone said, "What about the other six months?"

"Well, when it gets cold it has to warm up gradually. And that could take three months. Then when it starts to get hot, that could take another three months. That's going to take three months for each kind of weather to change." So they were thinking about it.

Just then the Coyote came back, and said, "You guys were talking while I was gone!"

"*Nooo*," they said. "We were just waiting for you to bring your pipe." Then they started talking about smoking again.

They said, "You didn't bring your tobacco!" One of the animals said, "Well, I think Coyote should bring his tobacco, because he makes good tobacco. You should have brought your tobacco when you brought your pipe. You have a *real* pretty bag for your tobacco. Yours is the most beautiful bag, the one you keep your tobacco in. And when you take it out, we like to look at it, because it's *sooo* beautiful. You always fix your tobacco good. It doesn't burn your throat."

So Coyote got all puffed up again, and ran back to his house a second time . . . And while he was gone the second time, they all agreed there would be four seasons. While Coyote was gone, they all said, "That is how it should be!"

So Coyote took off again, and went back to his house to look for his tobacco bag, to show it off—because he was a *big* show off. And while he was gone, they all said, "Is that how it should be?" Then Wolf told them, "We'll have three months each season: three months *tomo*—that's winter; and three months *tamano*—that's spring; and three months *tatza*—summer; and three months *yabano*—fall time. Is that the way everybody wants it to be? And the months when it gets too cold, all the animals that don't like the cold will go back in the ground and go to sleep. Then when the springtime comes, they'll wake up and they'll come back on the land. And when that happens, the bear's coat is going to get thinner, so he can stay here in the warm time, too."

Everybody shook their head in agreement. And Wolf, since he was the leader, said, "From now on that's the way it's going to be. All the animals will have their time throughout the year to be on the earth. And things will change in each season, the way I said. So that's the way it's going to be."

Then everybody started going back over the hill, and started going down the hill, walking back to the village. Then, as they were walking back to the village, Coyote came running back with his buckskin tobacco bag. He came running back and said, "Where's everybody going? Wait, *wait*. We've got to get back together again. We never talked yet! You guys can't do this without me!" But everybody just walked past him, walking back to the village. He told his brother Wolf, "We can't do this! We haven't smoked yet!" But his brother Wolf just walked on past him too, and back to the village. So that's how we got three months for each season, because of Wolf.

Wolf said, "That's how it's going to be." And that's how all the animals know what month to be awake, and what month to be asleep, and when their hair is going to get long, and when they start losing their hair, to get ready for summertime. Even the plants know when they have to come out of the ground and be ready for the animals to eat them. That's how everything fell into this form and into those four seasons, because the animals made the seasons. They voted on it a *looong* time ago. So that's how the seasons came to be.

# When the Animals Were Still People and Starvation Hit the Land

This is a legend from a *looong* time ago, when the animals were still people and when they were all over the land. Then a time came when starvation hit the land. They tried to go hunting, the people tried to go hunting, but they couldn't find anything. And they'd go fishing and they couldn't catch anything to eat.

So they came to see Wolf and said, "What are we going to do? We're starving! There's nothing for us to eat! You have the power to help us. What are we going to do now? How are we going to find food?"

Wolf told them, "I want four people to come forward." And four stepped forward. One was a Grizzly Bear, one was a Mouse, one was a Deer, and one was a Raven. And Wolf told them, "I want one of you to go to the north." So he sent the Grizzly Bear to the north. He sent the Deer to the east. And he sent the Mouse to the south, and the Raven went to the west. He said, "You should go as far as the land continues and then come back." And he continued, "You might find some food some place, and then you'll come and tell us, and we'll go there."

So they waited and waited, and the people kept dying. They waited and the babies were starving and crying. And the mothers were crying because their babies were dying. So they came back to Wolf and asked him, "When are they going to come back? What if something happened to them?" Wolf told them, "Don't worry, don't worry about them. They're going to come back."

Pretty soon the Deer that went to the east came back and told them, "I went *clear* over there, to where the sun comes up." Deer continued, "I went clear to the end of the earth. There's water there, nothing but water. And there are lots of plants over there. But I couldn't go farther and I didn't find anything to eat." Again the people waited.

Soon Raven came back from the west, and the people asked him, "What did you find over there?" Raven said, "I went clear to the west where the sun goes down, and I came to the water. And I went clear up toward the north and I went clear down toward the south, and there's nothing but water all along the land. As I came back the land there was full of trees, all kinds of big, tall trees. But there was no food!"

Again they waited, waited for the other two to come back. As they waited more people died. So the mothers came back to tell Wolf, "Our children are dying and we have nothing to eat. We need your help!" Wolf said, "We have to wait until the others come back."

The people began to lose hope. And they started to worry that maybe they were all going to die, maybe they were all going to starve to death. All of a sudden one of the people exclaimed, "Someone's coming!" What they heard was Grizzly Bear coming back. He was making a noise, *hrgh, hrgh, hrgh*, like he was running. They said, "The Grizzly Bear is back!" And the people all rushed to meet him. Wolf asked him, "What did you find up there in the north?"

Grizzly Bear told them, "You'll never believe what I found. I went up there to the north and there was a *big* mountain of ice. Because it was so huge I could not go around the mountain." Grizzly Bear told the people, "I first followed that ice wall clear to the east, and it went into the water. Then I came back and followed it clear to the west, and again it went into the water. But I still wanted to see what was over and on the other side of that mountain of ice. So I tried to crawl up and over the side of the ice mountain. But every time I started going up I would slide back." One of the people said, "Oh, I don't believe you. I think you're lying to us. The other animals went out, and they said that we were surrounded by water. Nothing could be that big."

So Grizzly Bear said, "Well, come with me then, and we will all see." So they all went to the north. All the animals packed up and went to see the mountain of ice. When they were approaching from a distance they could see white, and somebody said, "It's snowing! That's all it is, it's just snowing." And the Grizzly Bear told them, "We still have many more days to go." So they went on for many days, until they finally got to the wall of ice. And they looked up and it was true!

In awe, they looked up into the sky, and the ice mountain went up into the clouds. Eagle said, "I'm going to go up there. I'm going to fly up there to see what's above that ice." So he spread his wings and flew upwards. As he went farther and farther up he got smaller and smaller and smaller. After a while he started getting tired. Then he began flying in a circle, until he turned into just a little, tiny dot . . . and then he disappeared into the clouds.

He was gone for a *looong* time and the people got worried, saying, "What if something got him? What if he got stuck in the clouds?" So they waited for him to come back. Having never seen a mountain this huge and cold, they all touched it with their hands. It was cold! Some of the people tried to crawl up the side, but they'd slide back down. All of the animals that had claws, the squirrel, the badger, the cougar, they all tried to climb the ice. But they all slid back down. Then the deer tried to chip away at the ice with his horns. But he could only go so far before he gave up.

Then somebody said, "Look! The Eagle is coming back. Our brother is coming back!" Everyone was excited! They were all happy as the Eagle circled downward to earth. Around and around and around he came. He kept coming down until he got back to the place where the people were gathered. Since Wolf was the leader, he asked Eagle, "What did you see?"

Eagle told them, "I flew clear up through the clouds, until I couldn't see you down here on the earth. But I continued to fly *way* up above the clouds," he said, "to the top of the mountain." "I flew to the east where the mountain goes into the water, and to the west where it goes into the water. It's true what my brother, the Grizzly Bear, said." Eagle continued, "So I flew over the mountain, but there's nothing there but white, just snow and more ice. There is nothing growing there. As I flew and I flew and I flew, I started to get too cold. So I turned around and came back. There's nothing there for us to eat."

All the people were very sad to hear what Eagle said.

After what seemed a long, *long* time, Mouse finally came back from the south. When Mouse left for his journey he was really big, as big as the other people. When he got back he had traveled so far and grown so small that they didn't recognize him at first. Then the people asked him, "What did you see there in the south? What did you find?"

Mouse replied, "I went clear to the south and that was a warm place. I kept going and came to some mountains. I followed the mountains and I came to water, and water is all across the south. Then I came back. That land is *big*." Because he went far to the south, the Mouse took the longest time to come back. But when he came back and he brought back seeds!

When the people saw that Mouse brought back those seeds, they decided to go to the place where the seeds came from. So Mouse took them there. Mouse said, "We're going to go there. We're going to a place where there are giants. They have big baskets and keep their seeds in a cave." Then Wolf told all the people, "Get ready, we're going to go. We're going to get some more of these seeds." So they all got ready and left.

Mouse told them that the giants that have the seeds are a really fierce people. He continued, "They are fierce giants. And they can see over the mountains, so they might see us coming. So we have to be real sneaky." So they left.

As they were traveling Wolf told them, "Our brother Mouse is going to be the one to get more seeds for us. Then, once we get the seeds, if they start chasing us we'll have to give it to somebody else. Who will carry the seeds next?"

Magpie said, "I'll carry the seeds next. Mouse can give it to me and I'll take off with it."

Then Deer spoke up, saying that if Magpie gets tired he would carry the seeds next, by putting them in between his horns.

So they went on to that place where the *Pahizoho'o* stayed. They were the real fierce people that had the seeds. In the evening time the *Pahizoho'o* would build their fire and go into their cave. There they'd take some seeds out and grind them up and put them in a basket. Then they'd put water on them and stir them up into *pappe*, pine nut soup. Then they'd eat it.

When the people got to the *Pahizoho'o* village, they snuck around to find the pine nuts. Then Mouse went into the cave and looked in the basket—and to his surprise, there was only one seed remaining! But the *Pahizoho'o* knew how to make the seeds multiply when they needed to eat.

When Mouse put that seed in his mouth one of the giants who guards the seeds saw him and yelled, "Someone got the seed!" Mouse took off running, zigzag, throughout their camp, while they were trying to step on him and hit him with something. But they kept missing him. So Mouse took off and they all ran after him. Mouse kept running and running until he started to get tired.

That's when Magpie flew down, and Mouse handed the seed to him. Then Magpie took off flying with the seed, and Mouse jumped in a hole and went down into the ground. The *Pahizoho'o* then chased Magpie. He kept flying, and the monsters kept chasing him.

After a while Magpie's wings got tired, so he called out to Deer. Then Deer came and Magpie dropped the seed between his horns. Deer kept running, and the giants kept chasing him.

Finally Deer got tired and passed the seed to Coyote. Then Deer ran up in the mountains and hid in the trees, and the monsters ran past him. They continued to chase Coyote until he was utterly exhausted.

As the monsters got closer to Coyote he decided to play dead. He made his flesh dry up and smell rotten. He made his hair look matted. And he relieved himself on the surrounding ground. Before he lay down to play dead, Coyote hid the seed in a hollow leg. So the *Pahizoho'o* were deceived when they came upon him. They poked at him with a stick until some of his flesh came off.

In this way the *Pahizoho'o* were deceived and gave up the chase—and the animal people ended up with the only pine nut seed left! And Coyote gave the seed to his big brother, Wolf, so he could "use his power" to make more food.

## LEGEND 6

# Wolf Makes Pine Nut Trees

One day Wolf and Coyote were walking along in the mountains, and Wolf would talk to himself. Then he would spit. Wherever Wolf spit, a pine nut tree would grow.

After many days Coyote said, "I want to know how to that."

"No!" exclaimed Wolf. "You don't need to know how to do this."

The next day as they were walking together again, Coyote asked to learn how Wolf made the pine nut trees grow. Again, Coyote begged, "I want to do that. Let me try it." But Wolf again said, "No! I don't want you to do this." And when Coyote wasn't looking Wolf would spit, and *another* pine nut tree would grow!

As time went on Coyote continued to beg, "I just want to try it once." Each time they went for a walk together Wolf would spit, and pine nut trees would grow. But Wolf wouldn't tell Coyote how to do it, or let him have the seed.

Then one day Wolf got tired as they walked, so he lay down. But he was very concerned that if he fell asleep he might swallow the seed. So he took it out of his mouth and decided to keep it in his hand. Soon he fell asleep, and his hand opened and the seed rolled out.

Coyote immediately took the seed and put it in his mouth. And he boasted, "I can do anything my big brother can do!" Then Coyote snuck away from the place where his brother was sleeping. He didn't want his big brother Wolf to know what he was going to do.

Soon Coyote spit—and, surprisingly, where he spit a *juniper* tree grew! Oh . . . Coyote was *mad*. He said, "I did something wrong!" So he moved farther away from where his brother was sleeping and spit again—and *another* juniper tree grew! This happened again and again and again.

Soon Coyote was so mad that he started running around and yelling. He asked himself, "What did I do wrong?" Coyote thought to himself, "Wolf tricked me, I *know* he tricked me!" "He did this on purpose," he said angrily.

With all the commotion Wolf woke up and looked into his hand, and the seed was gone! Wolf got up and hurried to Coyote. Wolf scolded his little brother, "I told you not to do that. You're going to ruin everything!" Coyote snapped back, "I don't want this old seed anyway." And when he spit the seed out it grew into a big juniper tree.

Then Wolf commanded, "From this day on, no more pine nut trees are going to be made with magic. They will only grow where I have placed them." Today, that's why Oregon has lots of juniper trees, and Nevada has lots of pine nut trees.

The old people used to say, in the time of our people starving, if they could find where there were lots of mice they would be able to find some kind of food, because the mice know where the food is. So that's how we learned that from the Mouse. Even though Mouse was smaller than the deer and the elk and all the other animals, he saved the animal people.

## LEGEND 7

# "Animal Village," Lady Bighorn Sheep, and a Mother Turned into Stone

I once went to my grandma and asked her, "You've talked about Smith Rock being the 'Animal Village'—so what do you mean by that?" She told me that a long, long time ago, in the distant past, Smith Rock was an Animal Village. She said, "All the animals used to live there—elk, deer, bears, eagles, hawks, groundhogs, ground squirrels, and both bighorn sheep and mountain sheep, antelope—all the animals that are from our area, they all lived here at this place." She said that in the time of legends they all lived in the valley, between the two hills at Animal Village. That's where their houses were.

There was an old lady at Animal Village, and she had five sons. She was a Bighorn Sheep, *Koepa*. Then one year a time came when there was no food and the people were getting hungry. Her oldest son said, "Well, I'm going to go hunting." He told his mother, "I'm going to go hunting. I'm going to go a long ways because there's nothing to kill and eat around here. So I'm going to go a long ways." She told him, "You be careful! Take care of yourself!" So he left. He was gone for a *looong* time, and she got worried about him. She thought to herself, "What if *Nuwuzo'ho* gets him; then he won't come back!" She worried about him and worried about him, and their food was getting less and less.

Finally, the second oldest brother told her, "I'm going to go look for my brother. Maybe something happened to him. So I'm going to go." She said, "No, give him time. He's smart. He knows how to hunt, and he knows the land. He'll come back." And he said, "But he's been gone too long. Something might have happened, and he might be hurt. I'm going to go look for him." So he went off, in spite of her feelings. He left and he was gone.

Then she waited and waited more. And the other animals would come to her and ask, "Where did your son go?" "He went to look for his brother." "Well, they should have been back by now." So she got more worried, because the other animals were getting worried, and because her sons were good hunters. They knew how to get along out in the wilderness.

Then the third brother, who was a teenager, said, "I'm going to go look for my brothers." And the mother said, "No, you're too young." He told her, "Well, my brothers taught me how to hunt. They taught me all about the land, how to look for danger, and how to take care of myself. Maybe my brothers need my help." So he left, and he, too, was gone for a long time. She got so worried that she would get up early in the morning and face the sun rising in the east. She would cry and talk to the sun: "Father, where are my boys?" "Where are they?" "Did something happen to them?" "Did they die?" And she would pray to the sun, "Bring my boys back to me."

Then the fourth son, a young teenager, would hear her crying, and felt bad. So he told his mother, "My brothers should have been back. I think I'm going to go look for them." She told him, "No, you two are the only boys I have left now, and you can't go. If something happened and they're gone I'm going to need you boys here." "But we need food. We need something to eat. We're getting low on food. And I have to go look for my brothers." So he left for the east, too.

His mother cried for him, and because she only had her last, youngest boy left. Many days went by and there was no word from her sons. So she would get up in the morning and face the sun and pray to the sun. She would pray, "Father, hear me. My boys haven't come back, and I fear something has happened to them. Bring them home safe, take care of them."

Her youngest boy heard her crying early in the morning and felt bad because she was crying. And the animals would come to see her, and ask, "Where did your boy go?" She said, "He went to look for his brothers." They said, "Oh, my, I hope nothing happened to them!" Then she would cry more. And they'd put their arms around her and tell her not to feel bad, and that maybe they were all going to be safe and come back together. Maybe they got a lot of meat and are loaded down, and that's what's taking them a long time. "They'll be coming home," the animals assured her. And as she thought about it she got to feeling better.

Then the youngest boy left. He knew that if he asked his mother for permission to go she would tell him no. So he got up early one morning and left on his own. She missed him right away and started crying. She thought to herself, "I'm going to crawl up on the hill. I'm going to look for my boys. Maybe they're coming back."

So she went up the hill. She grabbed her rabbit skin blanket as she went up the hill, because it was windy up there. When she reached the top of the hill she wrapped her blanket around her neck and sat up there on a rock, looking to the east for signs of her boys.

The animals down in the village would look up at her and say, "Ooooh, that poor thing! All her sons are gone, and she's up there looking for them. But they're not going to come home. *Nuwuzo'ho* probably got them. They'll never come home." But some of the animals said, "Well, we don't know that. We're going to have to go up there and be with her. We shouldn't be like that." So some of the animals went up the hill to be with her.

Badger went up the hill and sat with her for a while. He said, "Your boys will come back. Maybe they're bringing back a lot of meat. Maybe they have a lot of food and need help. They're going to come back." Then badger came back down to the village. When he was up there he tried to tell her to come back with him, saying, "Come back down to the village. You must rest. You must sleep." The woman responded, "No, I'm going to stay here until my boys come." Then Badger went back down to the village, saying, "Oh, that woman—she's not going to come back down. She's not going to listen to anybody."

Then Weasel thought, "Well, I'm going to go up there." So he went up next. When he got to the top he sat by her and asked, "Are you doing okay?" "Yes, I am," she said. "Well, your boys are probably coming some place, so you should come back to the village with me." "No," she said, "I'm going to stay here and look for my boys. I want to see if they're going to come home." So Weasel sat up there with her for a long time. Then he got tired and came back down the hill to the village. "What did she say," the people asked. "She said that she's not going to come back down, that she's going to stay there until her boys come home." "Oh, that lady," they said, "Her boys might be dead, in which case she'll be sitting up there all the time." So they waited in the village.

Then Ground Squirrel decided, "I'm going to go up there and talk to her." So he went up the hill and sat by her. And they talked and talked. And Weasel also tried to tell her to come back down to the village. But she wouldn't come back down. So Ground Squirrel sat there with her for a long time. Finally Ground Squirrel got tired and came back down. He said, "She's not going to listen to anybody. She's just going to stay up there worrying about her sons, and waiting and looking for her sons."

Next, Lizard was going to go up to be with her. But when he got partway up the hill he heard her crying and was afraid to go on up. So he just lay there on the side of the hill, looking up at her. He didn't go all the way up.

Then Chipmunk decided to go up to her. And while he was going up the hill they all heard a big noise from the west. So Chipmunk turned around and started making all kinds of noise, shouting, "There's somebody coming from the west! There's somebody coming from the west!" Then all the people from the village came up the hill—the Badger, the Squirrel, and all of them, they all came up the hill. And the lizard turned around and was looking toward the west. They thought, "Maybe it's her boys coming back and making a lot of noise bringing food and everything." And Chipmunk was running around saying, "Big noise! They're coming! Somebody's coming from the west!"

Weasel ran halfway up the hill and was standing there looking. He stood up on his back legs looking toward the west, to see if somebody was coming. Then the old Badger crawled up next to the woman and told her, "They say there's somebody coming from the west." The wind was really blowing hard, so she held her rabbit-skin blanket, or *wea*, and pulled it over her head.

Coyote was watching all of this and thought to himself, "Those foolish people they keep going up there to be with that old lady. But she won't listen to them. She won't listen to anybody. Those people are foolish to think they're going to change her mind." So he went to the village and tried to call the people down. "You guys come down, come back down." But nobody came. They just said, "No, there's a noise, there's a noise." They were all up there toward the hill, excited and looking west.

So Coyote got mad at them. That's when he said, "Oh, those foolish people! They don't know what they're doing. There's nothing coming from the west—it's just the thunder from the clouds!" Then he tried again to call them back down, telling them, "It's just thunder, just thunder coming. Never mind that, come back down!" But they just looked at him and kept on looking to the west. And Coyote got *really* mad at them, because they wouldn't listen to him.

When the people went up on the hill they left the food they had in their baskets. So the Coyote ate all he could eat, so that people couldn't come back to the village. Then he emptied all their baskets and scattered all their food, throwing it up into the hills. That's why today you can find all the roots growing around this place. Bitterroot and desert parsley, and *haape*, all the roots our people eat. And all the seed foods, *wye* and *atsa,* and the juniper berries. They all grow on this mountain because this was Animal Village.

Then Coyote told them, "Well, if you guys want to stay up on the hill, then you are going stay there all the time." And one by one, including the ones that didn't go up on the hill, and the ones that wouldn't come back from the hill, he turned them all into rock. They're still up there today, all turned into rock.

# The Epic Battle of the Giant *Nuwuzo'ho* and Coyote—Fort Rock and Monkey Face

A *looong*, long time ago animals were the people on this earth. There were all kinds of animal people and other beings on the earth. There were those that lived under the water. There were flying beings. There were animal people across on the land. And there were giants that walked the land during this time. Our people called the giants *Nuwuzo'ho*.

There were also a lot of people spread out across the land and in villages all over the country. And in that time of the huge giant *Nuwuzo'ho* walked across the land. He used to walk with a long stick. It was about as long as he was tall, and it was sharp at one end. And as the giant would walk across the land he would look for people to eat. When he found a village, or a lone traveler or a hunter or some woman out gathering roots or berries, he would spear them with his long stick.

*Nuwuzo'ho* used to carry a big basket on his back. And he had a grinder, a pestle, inside of that basket. When he would stab the people with his sharpened stick, he would put them in that rock bowl on his back, until he had gathered enough to eat. Then he would stop and take that rock bowl off of his back. And he would take the pestle out and grind the people he had captured all up, bones and everything, mixing everything together. Then he would eat that mixture. Just like soup, he would eat them all.

When *Nuwuzo'ho* walked across the land the people were very afraid. When they heard his footsteps it sounded like thunder, and they would become terrified that he was coming their way, and to their area. So they would all go to hide from the giant. Or they would try to run away and stay ahead of him. But there were fewer and fewer and fewer people, because the *Nuwuzo'ho* was eating up all the animal people.

Finally the animal people decided that they were going to ask for help from the Coyote, *Etsa'a*. "We should ask Coyote to get rid of the *Nuwuzo'ho*," they said, "because Coyote knows everything, and he might be able to find a way to rid this land of the *Nuwuzo'ho*."

Some of the people spoke out against that idea. They said, "Nooo, we don't like to ask Coyote to do anything. Because he won't do anything for you unless you give him something. That's the way he is. He's always like that."

Somebody else spoke up and said, "We shouldn't ask Coyote, because then he'll always hold that against us. He'll always say that we came running to him, and then try to make himself better or higher than us. That's just the way he is."

Then some others said, "Well, you're right. He's always a know-it-all. He always knows everything. And even when he doesn't know something and we help him, he'll say, 'Oh, yeah, I was going to say that.' Or 'I was going to do that.' On the other hand, we can't get rid of the *Nuwuzo'ho* on our own, so we need Coyote's help."

Finally, they decided, "Let's go ask Coyote." So they went to look for him, and they found Coyote wandering across the land. They told him, "We need your help." And he said, "I *knew* you guys were coming. I just *knew* it. I already knew you guys wanted something. So, what is it that you want me to do now?"

Then the animal people said, "You know the *Nuwuzo'ho* that walks across the land. He's killing and eating all of our people. Pretty soon, there won't be any of us left, because of the giant *Nuwuzo'ho*. We need you to get rid of him once and for all."

So Coyote thought about it for a long time, and then said, "Well, right now I'm real busy. I have to find food for myself. I can't take time away from that to help you folks."

The animal people all looked at one another puzzled. Then they looked back at Coyote and started begging him, "But we *really* need your help. If you don't help us pretty soon there won't be any more people left on this earth."

"Well," said Coyote, "that is a *really* big and hard job! What are you guys going to give me?"

Then some of the people that went to ask him for help started mumbling among themselves, "I knew it! I *knew* he was going to say that! He never does anything for nothing."

But the chief told Coyote, "I have a very beautiful daughter. You have seen my daughter before. If you rid this land of the giant, if you kill the *Nuwuzo'ho*, you can have my daughter for your wife."

Now Coyote was one that was always impressed and overtaken by beauty of the women. And he knew the chief's daughter was very beautiful. So he decided he couldn't turn his back on the people, because he wanted to have the most beautiful wife in all the world. So Coyote said, "I'll do it."

The people were very happy when Coyote said he would do it. And they all went back to their villages and said, "Coyote has agreed!" They went to their villages and happily told one another, "He's going to take care of it!"

Then the day came when Coyote made his plan as to how he was going to rid the world of the *Nuwuzo' ho*. So he first made a fire. He gathered a lot of sagebrush, dried-up sagebrush, and made a big fire, so that there would be a lot of smoke. Then he rubbed willow between his hands, and it made sparks. Then he used more sagebrush, worked and dried up. It caught fire quickly and fed the larger fire. Then as Coyote blew on the sparks it turned into a flame and started burning the big pile of sagebrush. And a big, thick cloud of smoke went up, just like Coyote wanted.

*Nuwuzo'ho* wasn't far away, and he started smelling the air. Sniff, sniff, *sniff*. "I smell smoke," he thought. Then he stood up. He had been lying down, but now he stood up and started looking *all* around the land. "Somebody made a fire," he said. "The people are making a fire!" So the giant grabbed his pointed stick and got ready to put the rock on his back. He turned around and called all around, "Where is that fire?" Then he saw the smoke. "There they are! I knew they couldn't live without keeping warm, so they made a fire." Then he quickly headed out in that direction.

When *Nuwuzo'ho* got to the fire, the only one there was Coyote. Coyote was sitting by the fire warming his hands. Then he turned around and rubbed his butt cheeks. Then he turned back around and warmed his hands again. And then the *Nuwuzo'ho* came up to the fire, and whenever he stepped down it sounded like thunder coming.

Coyote turned around and looked up and saw the giant standing there, and he asked, "What are you doing here, my friend?"

The *Nuwuzo'ho* responded, "Don't you know who I am?"

"Oh, I know who you are," Coyote told him.

"Then why aren't you afraid of me?"

"Why should I be afraid of you?"

*Nuwuzo'ho* said, "Because I could stab you with this stick and eat you for my breakfast."

Then Coyote told him, "You know, you've been killing a lot of people—and that has to stop. So I think we need to have a contest to see who's going to win. If you win, you can continue going about your business of spearing and killing and eating the people. But if I win, then you'll have to stop."

The *Nuwuzo'ho* bust out laughing, and said, "Ah, ha-ha-ha-ha-ha-ha-ha-ha-ha-ha-ha-ha. And what are *you* going to do, what's a *little* man like you going to do to a *giant* like me? What are *you* going to do to *me*? What could you even *think* that you could do to get rid of me?"

So Coyote said, "Well, we should have a race. We should have a race across the land and go to that far mountain over there, run around the mountain, and then come back again. And whoever gets back here first is the winner."

And the *Nuwuzo'ho* wasn't a very fast giant, and he knew it. So he thought to himself, "If I race the Coyote, I know Coyote is fast and very tricky. He already has something planned and I'm going to lose." So he said, "No, a race isn't a good idea. I don't want to race."

Then Coyote looked at him and said, "I know. Let's use that bowl that you're carrying on your back to see which one of us is the strongest. One of us will crawl in that bowl and then the other one will get the pounder, and then we'll throw it down as hard as we can. Then the other one will do the same thing. And whoever's the strongest will win the contest."

Now the *Nuwuzo'ho* thought to himself, "Coyote isn't stronger than me! He can't beat me in this contest. He'll crawl in my bowl and I'll hit him once—and that's going to be the end of him." So *Nuwuzo'ho* told Coyote, "That sounds like a good idea." So Coyote and the giant agreed on this contest.

Then the *Nuwuzo'ho* thought to himself, "But who's going to be first?"

Just then Coyote told the *Nuwuzo'ho*, "Why don't you go first, since it's your bowl?"

The *Nuwuzo'ho* looked at Coyote and wondered, "Why is he so hasty? Why is he being so quick to tell me to crawl in first?"

About the same time Coyote thought to himself, "I know. I'm the bravest and smartest man in the whole world. So I'll crawl in first."

*Nuwuzo'ho* kind of smiled and thought to himself, "Now I have him! This is going to be the end of Coyote forever!"

Coyote crawled up to the edge of the bowl and looked in, and said, "Boy, that's a *long* way down!"

"Well," said the giant, "you said you were going to go first, so go ahead. Get in there!"

Then Coyote looked up and pointed to a mountain to the south and said, "Is that smoke way over there by that mountain?"

The *Nuwuzo'ho* turned around to look in the direction Coyote was pointing. He put his hands up to shade his eyes as he was looking, and asked, "Which mountain?"

And while *Nuwuzo'ho* was looking the other way, Coyote quickly took off his skin and threw it down in the bowl. Then he ran and jumped off the edge of the bowl, but outside of the bowl. Then he quickly crawled into a hole, and pulled the sagebrush up and over himself. Then he made his voice go inside of the bowl, as he answered the giant, "Oh, I think it was that was just a cloud, that's just that small cloud passing by over there."

When *Nuwuzo'ho* turned back around, he looked in the bowl—and saw Coyote's fur in there!

Once again, Coyote threw his voice in the bowl, and said to the giant, "Remember now, only five times. That's all you get is five times to pound and grind with that stone."

So the *Nuwuzo'ho* grabbed his long grinding rock and picked it up and brought it down into his bowl with a tremendous blow—"Hough!" Then he ground it around, and pulled it up thinking, "That's the end of him."

Then Coyote made his voice go back in the bowl again. "Did you pound the rock down yet?"

Oh, but that made the *Nuwuzo'ho* mad! So he lifted the huge grinding stone up again, and brought it crashing down into the bowl. Then he ground it around in the bowl some more. When he looked inside and could see blood on the side of the bowl. "That's it!" he said to himself, "Coyote's finished!"

Then Coyote threw his voice from the bowl to *Nuwuzo'ho* again, and said, "Thanks, that *really* felt good! That's *just* where my back was hurting. Do it again!"

Now *Nuwuzo'ho* got mad, oh, he was *really* mad! So he lifted his grinding rock as high as he could. Then he *jumped* off the ground and came down as *hard* as he could. He hit the bowl again and again, and he ground it around.

Coyote kind of moaned and said, "Ohh, ohh, ohh, ohh! That's just where my back was itching. You've got to help me get rid of the itch on my back."

And the *Nuwuzo'ho* was furious. He picked it up the huge grinding rock and brought it crashing down on the rock bowl again. Then he picked it up the fifth time and slammed it down again, and he ground it around and around and around.

Then Coyote made his voice go in the stone bowl again, and said to the giant, "I was mistaken. That *is* smoke down there by the mountain."

Once again, the *Nuwuzo'ho* turned around to look for the smoke to the south. And in that moment Coyote came out of the ground and jumped into the great stone bowl. Then he put on his all-battered-up, bloody skin, and came crawling out of the bowl.

The *Nuwuzo'ho* turned around and looked to see Coyote crawling out of the bowl. He was startled to see that Coyote was still alive.

"Now, it's my turn," said Coyote. So the *Nuwuzo'ho* crawled into the great bowl and Coyote summoned *all* of his magical power, to give him the strength to lift that huge grinding rock. Then he picked it up and lifted it as high as he could over his head, and brought it *crashing* down into the bowl. He hit the *Nuwuzo'ho* right on the head, injuring him.

Oh! Then Coyote picked the grinding rock up again and hit the giant again and again and again. And when the giant hit the side of the great bowl one side of it cracked and broke away, and the *Nuwuzo'ho* rolled out onto the ground. He was dying of all his injuries. He rolled one way and then he rolled back the other way, again and again on the desert ground. And as he rolled he was bleeding from his head and his arms and his legs. Finally, he became very still. And Coyote walked up on his huge body, onto his chest, and looked at him. Coyote had won. *Nuwuzo'ho* was dead!

Coyote looked out across the land. And every place where the *Nuwuzo'ho*'s blood had dropped or splattered, the ground and sands of the desert were red. And on the other side, where he was kicking around and pushing up the earth, where he was crying and weeping, there were lakes and salt puddles all over the desert. And his massive bowl, now broken out at the side, remains and is known today as Fort Rock.

To this day some legends tell us that *Nuwuzo'ho* is still lying there in the desert sands and the hard rock around Fort Rock. They say that the *Nuwuzo'ho*'s body is still lying there in those red dirt hills—called the Connelly Hills—just to the south of Fort Rock. And on the west side, toward Newberry Crater, those hills all have red cinder dirt that was stained in the battle between the *Nuwuzo'ho* and Coyote, when Coyote killed the giant. To the southeast, beyond Picture Rock Pass, are Silver Lake, Summer Lake, and Abert Lake, created by the tears that *Nuwuzo'ho* cried as he died. Much of this water is too salty for anything to live in.

Our people also tell another version of this legend, with a different conclusion for *Nuwuzo'ho*. According to that version the white people have always known the most prominent rock feature at Animal Village (Smith Rock) as Monkey Face, and it became famous around the world as Monkey Face. But the Paiute legend regarding Monkey Face begins at a time of the animal people and the giant *Nuwuzo'ho*. He was a giant cannibal that wandered the land. He used to go across the land and look for smoke. He knew that where there was smoke he might find a village. So he would go to that place to hunt and gather people.

*Nuwuzo'ho* used to carry a long pointed stick, like you see people at state parks poking all the garbage with, and picking up the trash. *Nuwuzo'ho* had a long, pointed stick like that. And when the people would attempt to run away he would go around and spear all the people. He carried a big basket on his back. Then, when he'd captured a lot of the people, he would bring them back to Fort Rock. That is where *Nuwuzo'ho* used to take the people and grind them up, before eating them.

So the giant used to carry the bowl of Fort Rock in the basket on his back. It was a bowl he strapped on his back and used whenever he was collecting people. The Fort Rock you see today is the rim of that grinding bowl carried by the giant, a bowl that was broken by the force of the fight between

Coyote and *Nuwuzo'ho*, and that has since settled into the ground. The giant would kill people and throw them in the bowl on his back. When he got to a certain place, or back to Fort Rock, he would take off the basket and the bowl, and take huge grinding rocks and pound the people all up. That's when the people were disappearing too fast, and that's when Coyote challenged and defeated the giant.

According to this version of the legend, *Nuwuzo'ho* once saw smoke on the other side of a high rock ridge at Animal Village (Smith Rock). So he snuck up to look over there, over that ridge to a village of the animal people on the other side. Apparently he killed and ground up and ate some of the animal people there, the way he often did when he walked across this land. So when Coyote challenged and defeated and killed the giant at Fort Rock, Coyote then turned *Nuwuzo'ho* into rock—into Monkey Face. And he's still at Animal Village today, still looking over that ridge for the animal people below, and still looking out over the land he used to roam and terrorize. He'll always remain there as a giant defeated by Coyote and turned into rock.

That was how the Coyote defeated and got rid of the *Nuwuzo'ho* once and for all. The legend is a testament to Coyote's bravery in ridding the world of an evil giant that terrified the people and almost killed all the people on this land.

## LEGEND 9

# A Story of Hunting
# and the Patience of the Hunter

A long time ago there were human people all over this country. Then the time came when everything was changing. The animal people were made into only animals. The weather was changing too. In that time some of the lakes were starting to dry up, and some of the springs were drying up. And the people were having to go farther and farther to hunt or gather food for their use. So they were moving from place to place all the time. They were trying to find an area where they could stay, an area that would provide food for them.

As they were moving around and looking for a place to stay, some of the children got sick. So they stopped and set up camp. They found a spring where there was water, and set up camp. Eventually everybody in that family got sick. And because the mother was getting weaker by the day, the man couldn't go hunting. He worried and worried about his family, and what would happen to them.

Finally, he went hunting anyway. He left the little camp they had and went to find something to eat. He was searching for something to kill and bring back to his family, so that he could cook it for them and they wouldn't starve.

While he was searching he came to a big meadow near their camp. He stopped there and felt so defeated that he started to cry. And while he was crying a little voice talked to him and told him, "You keep going. You're eventually going to find something to bring back to your family, and I'm going to help you." The man was encouraged by that voice, and so he kept on going.

As he walked along the man found a little stream and stopped to drink the water. Then he kept on going. But as he continued on he heard the rocks move on the side of a hill above him. So he paused and got his bow and arrow ready. He put the arrow into the bow and was ready to shoot whatever it was that was making the noise.

As he was sneaking up to the rock slide to see what was making the noise, he kept peeking around. He looked to his right and to his left. And he stretched his neck up, trying to see what was making the noise. When he got closer, he saw a rattlesnake curled up in the rocks. As it was curling up it made the small rocks fall, and they were hitting the larger rocks— and that made the noise. The man was so hungry that he laid down his bow and picked up a rock. He was going to kill that rattlesnake for food for his family.

Startled, the rattlesnake looked at him and talked to him. The rattlesnake told him, "You don't want to kill me. My people have never done anything to your people! So if you kill me you're going to have bad luck, and your family will die." So the man put down the rock and the rattlesnake told him, "If you keep going, you are going to eventually find something to eat." Then the rattlesnake crawled into some other rocks, and down into the ground.

The man sat there on the boulder for a moment and started to cry again. But then he thought about what the rattlesnake had told him. So the hunter picked up his bow and arrows and started walking again.

The man kept on going until he got tired. Then he sat down again, because he was so weak from the sickness he had. And as he was sitting there he heard the nearby bitterbrush moving around. He could hear something moving around in the brush. So he thought, "Well, there may be a deer in those tall bushes over there." So he hunkered down again, now with his bow ready. And he started sneaking forward toward the big patch of bitterbrush.

As he was sneaking forward, he would peek all around. He would look to the right and then to the left, and scan *all* around him to see if he was missing anything. Then he'd stand up a little bit, and try to look over the tops of the brush, to see if he could see the horns of a deer or something. But he didn't see anything. So he went up to the bushes and saw a few little birds in there. They were all eating seeds from the bushes. And they were the ones making the bushes move, as they would fly from bush to bush to bush.

By now the man was so hungry that he picked up some pebbles. He was going to throw them at the birds, just to get something to eat. But the little birds saw him, and told him, "You don't want to kill us, because we don't have very much meat on our bodies. It's not going to do you any good. Even if you kill all of us, there's not going to be enough meat to keep you alive. So you should let us live. And if you keep going you are going to find something bigger than us to eat." Then the birds flew off.

The man dropped the pebbles to the ground. Then he sat down and started to cry again. As time went on he was getting hungrier. So he got his gear and started off again. And while he was going along he came to a little creek. As he was bending over the creek to get a drink of water, he heard something in the tall rye grass next to the creek. The rye grass was moving around. And because it was in the late fall the grasses were all dried up, and making a lot of noise! So the man grabbed his bow and started sneaking toward that rye grass.

As he was going along and looking around in all directions, he thought it might be a deer. Or it might be a groundhog, or *something* that he could kill and take to his family. So he looked all around, just like he had the other times. When he couldn't see anything, he stood up as he was sneaking along. Then he saw the mice! They were all gathering the seeds that had fallen down from the rye grass. There were *many* little mice there, gathering up seeds to take to their home for the winter. But the man was *sooo* hungry that he decided to kill the mice.

Pretty soon the mice saw him, and saw that he had a stick and was going to start clubbing them. The mice looked at him and said, "You don't want to kill us, because we are too small. You wouldn't be able to get any food from us." And the mice told him the same thing: "If you keep going you're going to find something to eat." So the man looked at them. All of the mice had their cheeks full of seeds—and they all ran away.

Then the man sat there on his knees and started to cry again. He sadly thought, "I've gone everywhere, and done everything I can to save my family. But I haven't killed anything!" He started to feel really bad. Because by now he could have had a rattlesnake. He could have had those little birds. And he could have had a bunch of mice to take back to feed his family. Each time he thought about it he felt worse, because he could have cooked *all* that for his family. So the man was really sad, because everything that he could have used for food flew off or ran away.

As he continued on, he was going through a little thicket and heard more movement. This time he didn't do anything because he thought, "Well, it's going to be something small, and they're going to tell me, "Don't kill me!" So he went to investigate, to see what it was. As he got closer and closer he didn't have his bow ready. Then, when he got real close—he saw that it was a mule deer! When it was sharpening its horns in a dead juniper tree it got tangled up and couldn't pull its horns out. It was locked in the tree! So the man put an arrow in his bow and shot it! He was *sooo* glad that he finally had something to take home to his family to eat. He took out his obsidian knife and dressed the deer out. He took the heart and made a little fire. Then he got a stick and put the heart on that stick. And he cooked the heart and ate the heart from the deer.

Then he got out his little water bottle, and he had water. Then he prayed to the Creator, thanking him for the patience that he had, and thanking the Creator for listening, for sending the little animals to talk to him. And he thanked the Creator for giving him that deer. After he regained some strength from eating the heart, he loaded the deer on his back and went clear back to where his little camp was, to where his family was. When he got there he got sagebrush and made the fire. When it got going he got other wood and put it on the fire. Then he got willow sticks and bent them over the fire, to cook the meat for his family. He also made deer soup for his family to drink. Then his family ate the meat and drank the soup from the deer he had killed, and they all got well.

That's why our people tell this legend today. We have beliefs concerning the kind of animals we can kill and eat. That's why young boys are told not to kill lizards and snakes, because we can't eat them. And we're not supposed to kill little birds, those little brown birds you see all over, because they're not for food. And we don't hunt mice. Our people believe that if we're patient, even if we are tempted to give up, we will probably be blessed by getting some bigger game if we are patient. Then we'll be happy because we have waited.

So that is why our people tell this story, so that our young men will learn what not to kill. And they will learn not to give up when they are out hunting, but to be patient and keep on going. That's why our people tell this legend.

# Old Lady Jackrabbit,
# Little Fat Jackrabbit Girl, and the Ants

A *looong*, long time ago Old Lady Jackrabbit lived in a village down by the river. And her granddaughter lived with her. When the springtime came, all the people would get up early in the morning and head out to go dig roots. And every morning Old Lady Jackrabbit would try to wake up her granddaughter, saying, "It's time to get up! The people are leaving!"

Then the granddaughter would stretch—oh, *oooh*—and move around. Then she'd turn over, and grab her blanket, and pull it up—and go back to sleep! Her Grandma left her alone for a while. But the spring was getting on and Grandma knew that pretty soon the foods would be no more.

One day Old Lady Jackrabbit went out early in the morning and cut the *tseabu*, rosebush. Then she went in and told her granddaughter, "Get up now! The people are already getting ready to go. You have to go get food for us, or we're gonna starve when it gets cold! I can't go. I'm too old to go that far with the people, because they keep going farther and farther from the village. Now you have to get up and go!"

The granddaughter stretched her arms, and she stretched her legs, and she was going to turn over again—when her grandma poked her with that stick. "I told you to get up," she said, "You have to go!"

"Don't poke me around."

"You need to get up now."

But the granddaughter just covered up her head with her blankets, and was going to go back to sleep . . . so her grandma hit her with that switch with the rosebushes on it. "*Oooww*," she said, jumping up. "What did you do that for?"

Old Lady Jackrabbit said, "You have to get up now! You have to go with the people to dig roots. We must get roots!"

"Ah, you *always* want me to get up," the granddaughter said. "I don't know why everybody always has to be doing things!" And she was sort of grumbling around.

Old Lady Jackrabbit told her, "Before you go, I want you to take this basket down to the river and get some water." Then the granddaughter got mad. So she got the basket, and she went down the hill to the river, and she got the water, and she brought it back.

But by then the people were already leaving, they were already *way* out of the village. So she got her bag and her digger and everything, and she was getting ready to go catch up with them. But she wasn't really lively. She was kind of a chubby, chunky little girl. So she was going along and trying to catch up with the people, saying, "I don't know *why* I have to go do this. Everybody will *share* with us." She was mad because she had to go. But her grandma was standing there with the stick in her hand and telling her, "Hurry up now! Go catch up with them. Don't fall too far behind, or you won't know where to go."

The Little Fat Jackrabbit Girl kept on going. But every now and then she'd look over her shoulder and see her grandma standing there! Finally, she reached a little hill and saw the people go over it first. When she got to the hill and walked over it, she turned around to see if her grandma was still watching her. She was still standing there! So she went on over the hill. And as she was walking down, she looked over her shoulder again—and saw that her grandma was *still* standing there!

But when she got *way* over on the other side of the hill, the Little Fat Jackrabbit Girl said, "Well, she can't see me now!" But she saw that the people were *way* ahead of her. So she said to herself, "I'm not going to go dig roots. The people will share with us." And by the time she got over there the sun was getting kind of high in the sky, and it was warm. So she started looking around saying, "I'm going to lay down and sleep a little while. Then I'll go on and dig some roots."

So she found a place to lie down, and she lay down to sleep. She was almost going to sleep when she heard some singing. Then her ears would move around, and she said to herself, "Huh, it sounds like somebody's singing." She listened more, and thought, "No, I think it's just the wind." So she closed her eyes and was almost asleep again . . . when she heard the same sound! This time she looked around, saying, "It *does* sound like singing!" So she sat up and kept listening. Her ears would move around like a rabbit's ears move around. Then she stood up and looked around, saying, "What's making that noise? *That's* not the *wind*."

She started looking for the source of the sound. She went this way and pretty soon she went that way. She wouldn't go back toward the hill, because there her grandma might see her. Then she went another way, and the sound started getting louder. Pretty soon she could hear it very clearly. But she still couldn't see anybody. Someone was singing their song, she thought, "They're singing here somewhere." So she kept looking around, trying to find where they were singing.

Then she looked down, and there was an anthill! All of the ants had their little baskets to carry things in, and they were all carrying them on their back. They were carrying all of their seeds and everything, and going down in the hole in the anthill. And they were all singing a song!

The Little Fat Jackrabbit Girl looked at them in surprise and said, "How come you guys are all singing?"

"Because," they said, "it makes the work go by faster."

"Work, work, work! That's what everybody says. Work all the time. Everybody always wants to work. I don't know why you guys sing a song while you're working." She was just making fun of them.

Then the chief of the ants came and told her, "Go away! Go away from here. Don't bother us! If you're not going to work, then leave us alone and go away."

Little Fat Jackrabbit Girl said, "Oh, you guys are funny. I'm going to lay here and watch you guys." She knew she was much bigger than them. So she lay down and put her hand on her shoulder, and was watching them. They were all stretched out in a line by their anthill. When someone came out, they'd go off. And when the others came back, they'd carry their food down the hole in the anthill. They just kept carrying their food, and they kept on singing.

The chief kept trying to send her away. But she wouldn't leave, so she watched them for a while. She was kind of plump. And she was all stretched out there in the sun, and it started to get pretty warm on her back. Pretty soon she said, "Oh, I'm going to go," and she went to look for a sage bush. She walked over where she had been before, because there was a great big sage bush there. She lay down in the shade of that sage. And because she was warm she fell asleep quickly. She was snoring away—and as she was snoring she'd open her mouth and she'd close her mouth.

But Little Fat Jackrabbit Girl had made the leader of the ants angry. So he called the Indian ant doctor to come. The ant chief said, "We're going to do something to her. Because she is going to rest for a while, and then she's going to come back and bother us again." So the ants went to look for her and they found her. She was still asleep, and she was still snoring.

The Indian doctor ant had medicine. So the ants went up by her mouth. And when she breathed in, the doctor ant would throw his medicine into the air, and she would breathe it in. Pretty soon she went into a *real* deep sleep. She was *really* sleeping.

When the sun started to go down Little Fat Jackrabbit Girl started to get kind of cold. She woke up and looked around, and the sun was going down on the horizon. Then she looked down at her shadow, and her shadow wasn't round anymore! She was kind of skinny in the middle, around her waist. So she put her hands around her waist and felt around. And she thought to herself, "Gee, how long was I asleep?"

Then she thought, "I better go dig something, a little bit anyway, or my grandma's going to be real mad." But when she was gathering her digging stick and bag to go, she heard the ants singing again. And she thought, "*Oh*, those ants. All they do is sing!" So she went over to the anthill saying, "I'm going to teach them a lesson." She went over where they worked.

As she was getting closer she could see a little smoke rising in the air. Then she heard the ants singing, and forgot about her shadow, because those ants made her *mad*. That's when she went over there and saw that smoke going out from their hole. And she saw them! They were all in a circle, like they were round dancing. They were all holding something above their heads, and dancing around the fire. And they were all singing. They were dancing around their fire and they were singing a song, and she could hear them singing. And the closer she got the more she could hear of their song. Oh, and then she *really* got mad at them!

So she looked around and found a stick, swearing, "I'm going to fix those ants." And when they all looked up, she was running toward them with a stick up in the air, ready to hit them. But all the ants took off and ran down their hole, carrying with them whatever they were cooking.

She didn't know what that was until she got up real close, and just before they ran down their hole. Then she noticed that it was her *intestines* they had! They had taken them out of her while she was in her deep sleep, and they were cooking them over the fire. And that's what they were singing in their song! They were singing, "Rabbit guts! Rabbit guts! We're going to eat some rabbit guts! Rabbit guts we're going to eat. Little fat girl! Little fat girl!" *That's* why she was so skinny—because they had taken her intestines out, and were them cooking over the fire!

When she got there she was enraged. The ants had already run down their hole to safety. But she had her stick. So she hit the fire to break it up, and she did everything she could to put the fire out—because she didn't want her intestines to be cooked! So she jumped on the fire with her feet, and was stamping out the fire and hitting it with her hands. But by then it was too late.

That's why jackrabbits aren't as fat and lazy as they used to be. They used to be fat and plump. But ever since this happened jackrabbits are skinny. And jackrabbits now work all the time for their food. They hop all over the land to gather food for themselves. And that's why they have black on their feet. They got that from jumping around in the ashes, trying to put the fire out.

## LEGEND 11

# Why the Badger Has Long Claws and Digs

A long time ago, after death was put on this earth, there were bones all over the land. They were scattered all over the place. One day Wolf became very concerned about the dead bodies that were all over the land. So he called a meeting of all the people, and they all came together. He said, "We need to find a way to put these bones somewhere."

Some of the animals said, "Well, we could put them up in the trees."

Another animal said, "No! Even up in the tree they're going to smell. And they'll fall back to the ground."

So they thought about it some more, and someone said, "Well, we could throw them into the water. Then we won't be able to see them anymore."

But many of the animals that drink the water protested, "No, we can't put them in the water. Because we will not be able to drink the water with bodies in there."

They continued to talk about what they were going to do with all the dead bodies and bones.

A little while later Badger told them, "Let me take care of all the bodies that are on this land." And all the animals looked at Badger, because he was a very, very bad animal. And they thought, "What could he do? He barely moves around on this earth." In those days, the badger wasn't a fast animal. And he had short claws. And he lived up in the rocks wherever he could find a place that was big enough for him to stay.

Badger knew they weren't going to give him a chance to show them what he could do. So he told them, "I'm going to leave now. But tomorrow when I come back I will show you that I can do what needs to be done." Then he left.

All the animals began to wonder, "What can he do? Did you see how he just waddled away from the meeting? What is he going to do?"

But Wolf admonished them, "Well, let's wait till tomorrow and see what our brother Badger comes back with."

Throughout the night all of the animals were very restless, because they had troubling thoughts about what Badger was going to do. They worried, "I wonder what he's going to do."

In the meantime, Badger went back to his house in the rocks. But before he got there he came upon the rib cage of one of the animals. So he broke bones off that rib cage and took them home. During the night he broke those ribs in half and tied them onto his fingers. He worked throughout the night to make sure that they were tight and would not come untied.

The next day Badger came back to the meeting. All the animals were gathered, because they were curious to see what Badger was going to do.

But before he came down to meet with the people, Badger got *ebe,* the magic white paint. He painted around his eyes with it. And he made white stripes down his back, using the magical powers of the paint to move fast.

As he went down the hill to meet with the people, they saw him coming. Many of the people were afraid of him, because they could see the white paint on his face and the long claws on his hands. Some of them didn't even recognize him.

When he got there, he said, "This is how I'm going to take care of the bodies when they die." And right before their eyes, he started digging. The dirt started flying up this way and that way, until the people couldn't see through the dust. Then, as he was digging, a huge whirlwind came over the place he was digging. And all the dust was blown away and cleared the air.

Then the people looked around, and wondered, "Where's Badger? He's gone!"

There was a pile of dirt by a hole, all around the hole Badger dug. So Wolf went over and looked into the hole. And while he was peering in Badger popped up, and said, "This is how I'm going to take care of the dead people, because I can dig graves for them in the ground."

Wolf, the leader, was so pleased at what Badger was willing to do that he changed Badger from his plain self. He allowed Badger to keep the white stripes on his face and back. And the bones that were on his fingers became his claws.

To this day, that is why you cannot find the bones of elk or deer or mountain sheep or coyotes or anything in nature. Because the Badger gathers up the bodies and the bones and buries them.

## LEGEND 12

# A Big Dance in the Village—the Vanity of Coyote and Why Badger Is Flat and Mean

A long time ago all the people were busy doing different things in the village. The chief of the village was Wolf.

When they finished digging roots and hunting and everything, the people wanted to have a good time. They wanted to relax and have some fun. So Wolf said, "In a few days we're going to have a big dance. Everybody will come together on this day, and we're going to have a big dance. So everybody get ready for that day!"

Everybody was happy, saying, "*Good*. We're going to have a big dance in three days!" And everybody was anxious: the kids, the adults, everybody. They'd all say, "Oh good! It's two more days and there's going to be a big dance. Everybody's going to have fun! I wish it would come faster!"

In the meantime, while they were getting ready for the dance all of the old people started making their paint, making different kinds of paint. Blue, green, yellow, red, white, and *all* different colors of paint. They made it to paint themselves up for the dance. They also got feathers to tie in their hair. They were all getting ready.

So when Squirrel walked by Badger's house, he asked Badger, "How you doing?"

Badger looked at him and said only, "Ugh!"

Squirrel asked, "You gonna get ready to go the dance?"

Badger shook his head. "No."

But Squirrel continued, "Everybody's going to be there. There's people coming from another village. There's going to be a lot of people there. It would be good to see those people."

"Ugh!" Badger responded, and grumbled around.

Finally the day came when the people were going to the big dance. First, they put up a pole. They always used to put up a pole in the middle of the place where they were going to dance, and then they would dance around the pole.

Coyote was getting ready. He was going to go to the dance, and he thought, "I'm going to look better than everybody else!" So Coyote went down to the river and took a bath. He bathed himself, came out of the water, dried himself off, and started combing his fur all over . . . fixing it up really nice. Then he got ashes and started painting himself up with the ashes. He put it on his hair to make it blacker. "When I go to the dance *everybody's* going to notice me," he thought.

Then the people made a big brush enclosure like they used to a long time ago. It was like a big corral, made out of brush. And they had that pole in the middle. Everybody was coming, and they had an opening where everybody would enter on the east side. At that time they made a narrow opening there.

Pretty soon they started singing their songs and everybody started dancing around the pole. Everybody was having fun. Then they would sing another song, and everybody would start dancing around the pole.

Coyote was the last one to arrive. He said to himself, "I'm going to wait until they already start before I enter." So somebody asked, "Have you seen Coyote? Is he coming?"

Someone said, "I don't care if he comes. He's just going to show off if he shows up here." And they kept singing and dancing around.

Pretty soon someone said, "I don't see Coyote here. Usually he's here showing off, being a big show off. Where *is* he?"

"I don't care if he comes!"

Pretty soon Coyote came walking through the village. He passed by Badger sitting on a tree stump. Coyote said, "Aren't you going to the big dance? It sounds like they're singing a lot of good songs over there."

Badger growled, "I don't know why anybody wants to go over there. *I'm* not going over there!"

"You ought to come over and watch *me* dance," said Coyote.

"Ugh!" Badger said, just making his noisy, grumbly sound.

Coyote just looked at him and kept on walking to the place where all the people were gathered for the dance. When he got there and walked through the entrance, everybody said, "Here comes Coyote!" He was all painted up, with feathers in his hair and everything.

As soon as he got there they started singing another song. So Coyote got out there and started dancing. He was really stepping high with his feet. And he'd turn around real quick, and all the feathers tied on him stood up and looked real pretty.

"Ohhh, gee," someone said, and everybody was making a lot of noise. They were all watching Coyote, and all the other dancers would move out of his way. Then the singers *really* started singing hard, and really started singing loud. Coyote was really going to town. Badger could hear them.

"Ohhh, gee!" someone said again. Badger could hear that too, and he wondered, "*Now* what's Coyote doing over there?"

Pretty soon Badger got more curious. It seemed like people made more noise with every song they sang. So now Badger got *real* curious, and he started walking over there. Even though he didn't really want to be where all the people were, he was going to go see what was going on. He just *had* to go see what Coyote was doing that was causing such a commotion and making everybody so noisy.

When Badger got there he started peeking in the doorway. But there were a lot of people standing there, and he couldn't really see much. So he tried to stand up and stretch his neck around. And he tried to look over the others. But he still couldn't see. So he started pushing through the crowd.

Because he was so grumpy all the time, people were kind of afraid of Badger. They'd see him coming and say, "Oh, it's Badger!" Then they'd step aside. So he continued to make his way in. They started singing a song and pretty soon everybody was glancing at Badger, and they would all move out of his way.

Then the people started singing another song. And they started paying no attention to Badger, because they started dancing again. Besides, Coyote was out there and he was *really* dancing. He turned this way, and all his feathers would turn in a different way and flutter around. Then he'd turn the other way, and all his feathers would go in the opposite direction. And he would bend down and stand up, and put his arms out. And he was all painted up. Everybody was just admiring the way Coyote was dancing, and Badger was just looking at him.

Coyote was really dancing hard—until all of a sudden, he farted! He was spinning around at the time, so that scent went out into the crowd, and they reacted, "Aaah!" Then he turned the other way—and he farted *again*. And the smell got even *worse*. With that everybody started toward the door, pushing and shoving to get out the door. That smell was just a terrible smell, just *terrible*. The people wanted out of there!

By then Badger was standing in the doorway. And he was kind of old. So when the people started pushing out the doorway to get away from that terrible smell, they knocked him over. Then everybody trampled over him, stepped on him and everything, as they ran out the doorway and left the dance! When they were gone, there was Badger lying in the doorway.

That's how come today Badger has two black eyes, and he's flat and mean. Because everybody stepped on him when they were running away from Coyote's war dancing and farting at the big dance. Now Badger is even meaner than he was before the big dance.

## LEGEND 13

# How the Stars Got Their Twinkle and Why Coyote Howls to the Sky

A *looong* time ago, Coyote was walking along one evening. Actually, he was on his way to go to the restroom. He got up and he was walking to go out into the sagebrush and go to the restroom.

Then he looked up in the sky and the stars were starting to come out. There were just a few of them at first, the way it happens. Then more stars came out. So Coyote started thinking to himself, "I wonder what makes all those little lights up there in the sky? At first it starts out with one or two. Then some more come out. And pretty soon they *all* start to twinkle. I wonder what makes that happen?"

So he did what he went out to the sagebrush to do. Then he walked up on a nearby hill. He sat down on a rock on the hill and was looking up in the sky. As the sun went down lower and lower in the west, the stars were coming out in the sky, just like he expected. "It happens every night," he thought. "All those little lights in the sky. I wonder what they are?" Then he got up and went back to his willow hut.

Coyote fell asleep and dreamed that he went to go see his grandma, the spider, Old Lady Spider. So the next day he got up and thought to himself, "I'm going to listen to my dream and do what it says." So he went to see the grandma, Old Lady Spider. He told her, "I need you to make me a long rope, a *real* long rope."

"What do you want a long rope for?"

"I'm going to do something, and I need a *real* long rope."

"Well, I can't be making a rope for you to do foolish things!"

"No, no, no!" said Coyote. "It's for something good."

She looked at him, "I don't know. Every time you do something, you get yourself in trouble."

"No, it's not going to be for something like *that*. It's going to be for something good."

She thought and thought about it, and finally decided to listen to him. So she told him, "Okay, I'm going to make you a rope. How long do you need the rope to be?"

He said, "I need a rope long enough to go up there in the sky, *all* the way up to the clouds."

She looked at him again and asked, "What *are* you going to *do* with that rope? Why do you want a rope that's *so* long?"

"Well," said Coyote, "I'm going to do something special, and I need a *real* long rope!"

She finally decided, "Well, he can't make such a rope. And whatever he's going to do, he is going to get in trouble anyhow. So, I guess I'll make the rope for him."

Coyote was very happy. He went back home and did other things. His grandma started making him a rope, because she knew how to make real strong rope. And when she was finished she sent someone to get him and tell him his rope was ready.

Then Coyote came and took the rope. And he got his bow and his arrows and left. He thought, "I need to get closer up to the sky."

Coyote knew where there was a mountain called Pine Mountain. So he went up on that mountain and looked up at the sky. Then he got an arrow and tied the rope to the end of it. Pretty soon, when the day started turning to evening, he drew the arrow clear back in his bow, and shot it up into the sky!

Then he waited. And pretty soon his rope came tumbling back down to earth and got piled up again. He thought, "*That didn't work!*"

Then he went over to a big juniper tree that had a fork in it. He put the bowstring between the fork in the juniper tree. And he put the arrow in it, and put the rope on the arrow again. Then he pulled the bow *way* back with both hands, and shot the arrow up into the air.

This time it went *far* up. And as it went he started getting scared, because his rope pile was getting smaller and smaller and smaller. Pretty soon he was almost out of rope—and then pretty soon it stopped!

He looked up, and the rope was hanging down from *way* up in the sky. So he grabbed the rope and pulled on it. But it wouldn't give, it wouldn't pull down. He pulled on it more, and it still wouldn't pull down. So he jumped up and grabbed the rope—and it held him up!

By now the sun was descending to the point where it was going to go down. So he started climbing up the rope.

And he climbed and he climbed and he climbed. He looked down, and the earth was getting smaller and smaller and smaller.

When he got way up there he could see the house where he lived, *way* over there. And he could see the people, starting to put sagebrush on their fires. So he kept crawling up the rope.

Pretty soon he could hear people above him talking, so he kept climbing up the rope. He knew that somebody was talking up above him, so he kept climbing up the rope.

Pretty soon he got to the bottom of a cloud, and he crawled through it. When he got up above the cloud he came out of the hole. He looked around, and there was land up there, just like on the earth.

So he crawled out of the hole. Then he could see that there was a fire, and there was somebody standing by that fire. So he started walking toward that fire.

When he got closer it turned out to be a lady. She was standing there with a dress on. It was decorated with abalone shells on the fringes. And every time she would move the firelight would hit those shells, and they would sparkle. Pretty soon another lady joined her. And as it was getting darker, still another lady joined her.

Pretty soon you could hear a lot of talking, as a whole bunch of people were coming. They were ladies. And they all had abalone shells tied *all* over their dresses, on their headbands, and on their moccasins and everything.

Then they started singing and dancing all around the fire. And when they were dancing *all* those abalone shells would sparkle.

As the Coyote was looking at them, he started getting shorter and shorter. He looked down, and realized that he was starting to sink into the land up there!

One of the ladies told him, "You're going to fall back through this land. You have to dance, or you'll fall through!"

So he started dancing, and he came back up! He started dancing with them, and they danced and they danced. Coyote liked being up there, because there were lots of pretty women. He didn't want to leave.

Then he got tired of dancing, so he sat down. But when he sat down he started sinking again! So he jumped up and started jumping around and dancing with the ladies again. And then he came back up on the land.

But he was getting more and more tired. And he said, "I don't know how I'm going to be able to stay up here! Every time I dance, I'm fine. But when I get tired and sit down, I start sinking! I think I might fall back to earth!"

So he danced over where the hole was, and he grabbed the rope, and he started pulling it up. There was a pole over where the ladies were dancing, and he thought "I'm going to tie myself to that pole. That way if I get tired and start to sink in, then I'll be tied to the pole!"

So he tied himself to the pole, and nobody said anything. And as he was tied to the pole the ladies were dancing, and he was dancing with them. That went on for four nights.

Pretty soon he got tired. By the fifth night he was so tired he just couldn't dance anymore. He *really* didn't want to leave those beautiful women. He wanted to stay up there and dance with them all the time. But his feet were getting tired. And his legs were getting tired.

Pretty soon they were building the fire for the dance. Everybody started coming out, and they were all dancing. But he was just exhausted. He was so tired that he quit dancing—and he started sinking again. He thought, "My rope is going to hold me this time. I won't fall back to earth. I'll climb back up when I get my rest."

But when he was sinking, the rope was pulled through the fire and caught on fire! Then he fell from the sky, with the burning rope trailing behind him—he looked like a falling star. He hit the earth at a place we now call Hole-in-the-Ground.

When Coyote stood up, he went up on Pine Mountain again. And he looked up at the sky and the clouds. He wanted to be up there with all those beautiful women dancing in the firelight. He wanted to be up there dancing with the women with the shell dresses on. He wanted to stay up there and dance with them forever!

He went back to his grandma Old Lady Spider again, and asked her to make him another rope. But she told him, "No. You would just use it for something foolish. I'm not going to make you another rope."

Coyote kept thinking about what he saw up there. And every night when the sun went down he would go up on the hill and look up into the sky. When the first star would come out and start twinkling, he would start crying "*howwuuu, howwuuu*!" And he would cry out, "I want to be up there, I want to be up there."

Soon more stars would come out. And the more stars that came out the more Coyote would cry out. He didn't want to leave all those pretty ladies up there in the sky, dancing around the fire, with abalone shells tied all over their dresses, sparkling in the firelight. That's how the stars got their twinkle.

Now every time the stars come out at night the Coyotes go up on the hills and cry out. They want to go back up in the sky and dance with the beautiful ladies dancing around the fire making starlight.

## LEGEND 14

# Why Porcupines Eat Willows
# and Cottonwood Saplings

A *looong* time ago, Porcupine was going along the river. He was trying to find a place with a really good stand of willows to eat. And he was looking for some nice, young cottonwood trees. As he was going along the river he was getting tired. That was because the side of the river he was on had great big cottonwoods and not too many willows.

As he was going along, he heard a snorting sound. So he was kind of afraid, because porcupines are afraid of cougars and he thought it might be a cougar. So he got scared.

As Porcupine was sneaking along the river and going through the grass, every now and then he would peek up, because he wasn't very tall. And when he looked up he saw some buffalo. They were near the edge of the river, eating the grass that was growing there.

And just about the time he saw those buffalo, Porcupine looked across the river and saw a *whole* bunch of willows and young cottonwoods growing on the other side of the water. So he went to make himself known to the buffalos. But as he was going to talk to the buffalos, he thought to himself, "Well, I would sure like to eat some buffalo meat." And he thought,

"If I can just get a great big buffalo to carry me across the river, then I'll kill him with my arrows, just when we're almost on the other side. Then his friends can't come across and help him." That was his plan.

So Porcupine walked up to the biggest Buffalo and said, "I need your help. I want to get to the other side of the river, but I'm too small."

"Why don't you swim across?" Buffalo asked him.

"Because I'm not a good swimmer," he said. "My legs are too short, and the river might carry me down, and I might drown. But if you would carry me across on your back I think I could get to the other side."

The Buffalo kept on eating the grass, and stepping forward as he ate. Then Porcupine asked him again, "Well, what do you think? Will you take me across?"

"Oh, why don't you go ask one of the other guys. They might take you across. I'm busy."

Porcupine looked at the other buffalos. They were too small, and one looked too scrawny and didn't have enough meat on him. So Porcupine said, "I'm afraid they don't look like they can swim very well. But you're *real* strong looking. I'd *much* rather have you take me across, if you will."

The Buffalo was getting tired of listening to him. But Porcupine continued to ask, "Well, what do you think?"

The Buffalo would take a bite of grass, and then turn the other way. But Porcupine would move around the other way and say, "I really want to go to the other side."

Finally, the Buffalo said, "Okay, I'll take you across. You get on my back." So Porcupine grabbed his tail and crawled up on his back, and the Buffalo started walking into the river.

When it started getting deeper Porcupine moved farther up his back, and was riding on his hump. When they got in still deeper the Buffalo couldn't touch the bottom, so he started swimming. Just his head was up above the water. So the Porcupine moved up to his head and said, "I'm afraid I might fall in! I might drown! I don't want to die!"

"Get between my horns," Buffalo snorted. So Porcupine moved up between his horns—and then things got even worse. "I'm going to fall off!" Porcupine cried, "I'm going to fall off! I can't ride between your horns."

"Hang on to my horns!" the Buffalo commanded.

"No! They're slippery and they're wet," said Porcupine. "And I might fall off."

"Then ride on my nose!" So Porcupine moved up on his nose, and Buffalo kept swimming across the river.

"I'm going to slip off your nose!" Porcupine cried, adding, "I have a better idea. Why don't you open your mouth and I'll ride inside your mouth?"

So the Buffalo opened his mouth and Porcupine crawled in there. And he looked out at the other side of the river. "I better not kill him yet," he thought. "Because if I kill him now we're both going to drown." So he waited more.

Even when Buffalo started walking on the bottom, Porcupine waited until he was almost out of the river. Then Porcupine pulled his arrows out and stabbed Buffalo in the throat! So when the Buffalo came out on the other side of the river, he bled and fell down on the bank. His buffalo partners back across the river were too small and weak, and couldn't come to save their leader.

Now the Porcupine was happy, because he had that *whole* Buffalo to himself. He wasn't wishing for willows or young cottonwood trees.

Then Porcupine took his obsidian knife out, and was going to start cutting Buffalo up and butchering him. All the other buffalo on the other side of the river were watching and saying, "Oh, *no*. He's going to cut up our leader! He's going to eat him!" And they would walk up and down the riverbank, trying to find a shallow place to cross. But they weren't big enough or tall enough to swim across the river. So Porcupine got his knife out and started cutting the Buffalo open.

Just about that time Porcupine heard somebody coming up the river and singing. "Uh, oh!" he thought, "Somebody's coming." So he crawled up in a tree and looked around—and there was Coyote coming up the river.

"I bet Coyote is going to want to take part of my kill. I don't want to share it with him!"

So Porcupine crawled down closer and started cutting willows and covering up the Buffalo. Meanwhile, Coyote was getting *closer* and *closer* all the time. Porcupine could tell because Coyote's song was getting louder and louder. Porcupine was really hurrying. But his little legs were short, and he ran around here and there, cutting willows and piling them up on the Buffalo. And just about the time it was almost all hidden, the Coyote came upon him.

"What are you doing, Porcupine?" Coyote asked.

Porcupine said, "Oh, I'm just looking for my knife. I dropped my knife and now I can't find it."

"Why don't I help you look for your knife?"

"Oh, no, no, no! I don't need your help. I'll find it."

"No, that's ok. I'm not in a hurry, and I can help you."

"No, I don't need your help. Go ahead and go on your way, I'll find it. I'm not in a hurry."

"No, I can help you look."

So Coyote started walking around through the willows and the grass. And every now and then he'd pause and lift up his nose. "I think I smell buffalo meat!"

Then Porcupine said, "There's some buffalo on the other side of the river. I saw them there. And I could hear them making noise. They were eating grass over there. They're probably still there."

Coyote looked around, but he didn't see any buffalo on the other side. So he kept looking for Porcupine's obsidian knife. "I'll help you look," he said.

Porcupine said "No, just go ahead. You can go on. I'll find it pretty soon."

While the Coyote was looking around he happened to see the Buffalo, all covered up with sticks and willows. Porcupine saw him getting closer and closer to the place where he had covered the Buffalo. And Porcupine told him, "I already looked over there. No need to look over there." He added, "Don't look over there."

Coyote said, "No, you might have overlooked it. It might be over here. I'll look." So he went over there and started peeking around.

"So *that's* why he doesn't want me here, Coyote thought. He has this *whole* Buffalo hidden over here. And he's going to cut it up to cook. I like buffalo meat!" So he walked around it.

Pretty soon the Porcupine called him and said, "Hey, look what I found. I found my knife. Now you can go."

The Coyote said, "When you found your knife, look what I found over here! There's a whole Buffalo over here. Looks like somebody killed a Buffalo and left it here—and I found it."

The Porcupine told him, "Well, I killed the Buffalo. That's my Buffalo."

"You're too little to kill that Buffalo," Coyote told him.

"No, I killed the Buffalo. I killed him with my arrows."

Coyote said "No, I think somebody else killed it. I think you are just trying to take it away from somebody else."

"No, I killed it."

"Well, if you killed it, then you have to share with me!"

Porcupine thought, "I don't want to share it with him!" Then he thought, "Well, how am I going to get rid of him? How am I going to make him go away?" So he thought about it.

The Coyote was watching him and knew he was trying to think of a way out of the predicament they were in. So Coyote said, "I'll tell you what. We'll have a contest, and whoever wins the contest will get the whole Buffalo."

The Porcupine thought about it and said to himself, "No, because Coyote's going to say we'll race, and Coyote has long legs and I'll get beat." So Porcupine thought about it and said, "What do you think we should do?"

The Coyote said, "Let's have a race."

So Porcupine thought, "It's just what I thought! He says we'll have a race!" Porcupine said, "No, I don't want a race, because you've got longer legs than me and you'll win. I've got little, short legs and you're going to beat me. I don't want to race." And he thought to himself, "I wonder what we could do."

Then Coyote told him, "Let's play stick game."

Porcupine thought, "No, because Coyote has magic, and I know he cheats. He doesn't play fair." So he said to Coyote, "No I don't want to play stick game because you'll use your magic and you'll beat me."

"Well, what do you think, then?" Coyote asked. "What do you want to do? Let's have a jumping contest."

Porcupine thought about it, "Well, if I can land on the willows, they will spring back and toss me forward, and Coyote won't expect that." So Porcupine said, "Okay, we'll do that."

Then Coyote said, "We'll jump over the Buffalo. Whoever can jump the farthest on the other side of the Buffalo will be the winner."

Porcupine thought about it and said, "Well, okay." And he thought, "I'll make the Coyote jump over first, so when he jumps over the Buffalo, he can't see me on the other side. Meanwhile, I'll put the willows there. Then when I jump on the willows, they will toss me *way* over the Buffalo. So he told Coyote, "Go ahead. You go first."

Coyote took off running. He went *way* back and took off running, and he jumped *clear* over the Buffalo, where it was laying down.

Then Porcupine really hurried around. He made a place where there was a springy, green willow, and went back far enough and said, "Here I come now." He took off running and when he jumped he *missed* that springy green willow, and hit a dry one instead. It busted and he just hit the side of the Buffalo, and flopped down on the side of the Buffalo.

So Coyote won the Buffalo. Then Coyote told him, "Okay, hey! I won! Now you have to go away and leave me alone to tend to my business."

And Coyote told him, "From this day on, because you wouldn't share the Buffalo with me, all you'll ever eat will be willows and cottonwood saplings. That's going to be your only food. You're always going to chew on plants."

So Porcupine went away. Ever since then Porcupines only eat willows and cottonwood saplings. And Coyote got the Buffalo and ate the Buffalo.

## LEGEND 15

# Black Bear's Gift of Roots and Medicine

A *looong* time ago there was a time when the land was changing. This was after the human people were put on this land. And the animals were being placed on the land wherever they were going to be for the rest of their time. The deer would be in the juniper thickets, and some of them would be up in the mountains. The fish were all in the water, the *Agi,* the salmon and trout, were all in the water. All of the animals were being given their homes, wherever they were going to be.

Sometime after they were all placed in the land, the land started to dry up. Some of the springs dried up and some of the lakes were disappearing. Where there were once nice and green meadows the grass was all drying up.

In this world there was a man and his family, his wife and his little baby. One day he went out to go hunting and find food for his family. While he was hunting he was going to try to find some plants for medicine, because his baby was sick.

So he went up into the mountains. When he was leaving from their camp his wife was pleading with him to hurry and not be away too long. Because the baby was so sick she was afraid it was going to die. It wouldn't even cry and its color was starting to turn pale.

So the man was trying to hurry. He went way up in the mountains, trying to look for something, for a deer to kill, so he could come back to his family with some food to eat. He was also looking for a certain kind of plant that our people used to dig and get for sickness. But he couldn't find it.

While he was searching around up there on the mountain he heard a noise. So he crouched down and went where he heard the noise. He was ready to kill whatever it was, and thought that it might be a Deer. But when he got there it turned out to be a Black Bear. The Black Bear was digging in the ground with her claws. It was a she-bear and she was digging at the base of a big pine tree, a rotten, dead pine tree. The Bear was digging out the ants that were living in there.

The man thought, "I'm going to shoot the Bear. It's big enough, and I'll use it for food." So he got ready.

At the same time, the Bear had power, and the Bear's power told her that the man was getting ready to kill her. So she stood up on her back legs. She raised her hand, her right paw, and told him, "Stop! You don't want to kill me, because I never did anything to you. Yet you want to take my life."

So the man told her, "If I don't take your life then my baby is going to die. My family needs food to eat."

The Bear told him, "Well, you don't have to kill me for food to eat!" Then she dropped down on her all four paws and she looked at him and said, "Follow me. I'm going to show you where to get food." So the man put his bow down. He didn't really know whether to trust her or not, soo he kept his bow ready to pull back if he needed to. Because he thought she was going to trick him.

So he started following her at a safe distance. When the Bear came to a small meadow she started digging in the ground, and pushing up a lot of dirt. She used her claws. And she told him,

"Here, here's food for you to eat, right here!" When he went over, there were little roots that our people call *yapa*, Indian carrots. So the Bear dug up the ground with her claws, and the man collected a whole bunch of those carrot roots.

Then the Bear told him, "Come with me, I'm going to show you something else." So the man gathered what he could and took off following her. They soon came to another place. And once again the Bear started digging around in the ground. She dug up some other kind of roots. So he gathered those roots, too. She told him, "You can eat this, this is for food. This is what I eat."

Bear did that three times. And each time the man gathered more roots. Then Bear took the man to another meadow. At the edge of the meadow she dug up some more roots, and told him, "You take this back and pound it with a rock. Then you mix it with water and give it to your baby—and your baby is going to get well! You breathe in the smell and your baby will no longer be sick! This is what I'm going to give to you, because you spared my life."

So the man went back down the mountain to his home. When he was still a ways off he heard his wife crying. So when he got there he thought his baby was dead. But the baby was barely living, barely hanging on. So he told his wife how to cook the roots, and she cooked them, and they ate the roots. And the man prepared the medicine, and fanned the steam toward the baby, and the baby was breathing in the medicine. Then the man made a little spoon out of a leaf and put it by the baby's mouth, and the baby drank the medicine.

Pretty soon the baby's color started to come back, and it started to breathe regularly again. And after a while the baby got well.

Later the man took his wife and his child to the meadows where the Bear had showed him where those roots grew. He told his wife, "This is where we dug, at this kind of a place." And he showed her what the Bear had said, "Wherever you see a place like this, this root is going to be growing there. If you look and dig, you'll find it."

Then they went on. When they got to the next meadow, it was a different kind of land. And the man said, "The Bear said that in this kind of place you're going to find this kind of a root. And you'll only find it in this kind of a place."

Then they went to the third place. And the man said, "In this kind of a land, this is where you're going to find this kind of root. That's what the Black Bear told me."

Finally, he took his wife and showed her where they got the medicine root, the medicine that saved their child. And the man said, "This is where you get this root. But you never take the whole root. You always just take part of it." They find that root on the hillside or at the bottom of the hill. Our people call that root *dosa*. It's a real strong medicine plant.

That's the legend my people tell of Black Bear's gift of roots and medicine.

# Coyote and the Escape of Mouse

A *looong* time ago, Coyote was walking across the desert. He was walking along through the sagebrush and rabbit brushes and junipers. And every now and then he would start trotting. So as he was going along he got kind of hungry and decided to look for something to eat.

So then he went this way. And then he'd turn around and come back the other way, kind of zigzagging through the sagebrush. Then when he came to a grassy area and he heard some singing. He stopped so his ears could hear it. And when he stopped, his ears would kind of move around, and he could figure out where the singing was coming from.

Then he kind of crouched down and snuck up on the sound—and there was a Mouse! It was gathering seeds, so its cheeks were *all* full of seeds. And it was running here and there to pick up seeds. Coyote thought, "Well there's my meal right there! I'm going to catch that little Mouse and eat it up."

So he snuck up real close. The Mouse didn't hear him coming because the Mouse was singing its song and gathering seeds, and it wasn't paying attention. So Coyote jumped and caught the little Mouse between his paws.

The Mouse was terrified, because he knew the only reason Coyote would be catching him was because he was hungry. So the Mouse was really scared and asked Coyote, "What are you going to do to me?"

Coyote told him, "I've been walking around all day long and now I'm hungry. So I'm going to eat you."

Mouse told him "No, you don't want to eat me! Please don't eat me! I don't want you to eat me, because I'm just a *liiittle bitty* mouse. I wouldn't even be able to fill you up if you eat me."

But Coyote said again, "I'm really hungry. So I'm going to eat you."

The Mouse kept pleading with him, saying, "No, you can't eat me. I'm too little."

Then the Mouse told him, "I'll tell you what. If you dig a hole and put me in that hole and cover me up, while I'm in the ground I'll start to grow. Then I won't be a *little*, *bitty*, *tiny*, *scrawny* little Mouse any more, but I'll get *bigger*. Maybe I'll become the size of a Jackrabbit. Or I might get big like a Groundhog!"

Coyote thought about it, and said, "No, I think you're trying to fool me. I think you're lying to me."

"No, really. You bury me, and I'll grow."

Then Coyote thought, "Well, he *is* kind of small." So he held the Mouse's tail with one paw and with his other one he dug a hole real fast. Then he picked the Mouse up and put him in the hole. And he covered the Mouse up, and laid down *right there*. He laid down *right* next to where he buried that little Mouse.

Coyote waited and waited. And he saw the dirt over the hole starting to push up in a little mound. "He's growing," Coyote thought to himself. "He must be getting bigger." So the Coyote waited and waited some more.

But while Coyote was waiting, the Mouse wasn't growing under the ground! The Mouse was digging a hole to get away! He was digging a little tunnel, and he came out some place else—and took off and escaped! Meanwhile, the Coyote was still waiting for the Mouse to grow big.

That's the legend my people tell of Coyote and the Mouse, when the Mouse was clever enough to fool Coyote and get away.

## LEGEND 17

# Why the Rat's Tail Has No Hair

This story happened a *looong* time ago. There were a whole bunch of people in their village. And there was one in the village that was *Tekawa*—the Rat. He used to always sit outside his house, and sit there close by the fire. And he had a comb made out of the roots of wild rye grass. So he would sit outside and hold his tail. And every day he would comb the *looong* fur on his tail. Then, when he finished combing it, he'd get up and walk through the village. And the breeze would blow on his tail and make it kind of wavy and flowing.

So he'd walk all through the village and the people would look at him. And when he first did that, the people would say, "Ohhhh, my! What a *beautiful* tail you have!" Then he'd stick his tail up higher, and more up in the air. And the wind would hit it—and his tail would just flow in the wind. And he'd walk through the village like that.

Pretty soon it got to the point where everybody just got tired of seeing him parade through the village with his combed tail flowing in the wind. They just got tired of looking at it. People would glance up and then just keep on doing their work, whatever they were doing, making baskets or making arrows or something. They wouldn't even notice him.

Then Rat would still go back to his house and sit down by the fire again. And he would get some kind of grease. He would heat it by the fire and put it on his hands. Then he'd rub his tail with it, and it would get real shiny. Then it would kind of dry a little bit, and he'd comb it some more.

Then he'd get up and walk around some more while it was still daylight. He'd walk around the village, and people would notice it. The kids would notice and they'd say, "Look, Mom! There goes the Rat!" The villagers would glance up and look—and then they'd turn away. They were just getting tired of him showing off all the time.

One day the villagers decided to have a big dance. And they were telling everybody, "We're going to have a big dance on this day. Everybody get ready to come to the dance. Everybody put on your paint." Because in those days the animal people use to paint their faces for such an event. They used to paint their faces with red paint, yellow paint, white paint, or black paint. So they'd paint themselves up real nice looking. Then they'd tie different-colored feathers on their hair or on their fur. Or they would make things out of shells to hang from their neck. Or they would put on round bracelets that were made out of shells. That way they would all get *all* ready for the dance.

But the Rat said, "I don't need to do that, I have *such* a beautiful tail. *Everybody* will admire my tail when they are dancing. I'll just put the grease on it and comb it, and it'll look real shiny. And when the wind blows it'll make my tail move around and everybody will say, 'Oh, look at his tail, it's so pretty!'"

As the day was approaching, everybody was just *tired* of Rat showing off all the time. Then the Ants came up with an idea. They said to themselves, "We'll show him about his tail, and always showing off!"

One day well before the powwow the Ants started a rumor in the village: that the Ants know how to fix your tail so it will look *much* prettier than *anybody* else's tail! Soon the people were talking and whispering about that rumor, until it finally reached Rat's ears. "*Ohhh*, so the Ants *do* know how to fix my tail! I will ask the Ants to fix my tail!"

So the Rat called for them to come and talk with him. But the Ants said, "*Nooo*, we're too busy! We're real busy!" And people were all talking about it.

Pretty soon Rat went to see them again, saying, "I need you guys to come. I want to talk to you!"

"Well," the Ants said, when we're finished doing our job, we'll come talk to you."

Then the Rat went home—and the Ants never came back!

But the animal people were still *determined* to have the big dance. And the day of the dance was drawing *closer* and *closer*. So now the Rat *really* wanted to get his tail fixed.

Then the Ants went to Rat's house and told him, "We're going to fix your tail for you. But you can't watch us. You can't watch what we're doing! We're going to fix your tail so that it's even more beautiful than what you can do to it. It's going to be *so* beautiful that *everybody* will admire it."

And oh, that sounded *just right* to Rat. So he said, "Okay!"

Then the Ants said, "Remember now, you can't turn around and look while we're fixing your tail! Because if you look we might make a mistake, and then we're going to ruin it."

The Rat responded, telling them, "Okay, but there is one thing you guys *can't* do."

And the Ants said, "What's that?"

He said, "You cannot cut *any* of the hair off my tail!"

The Ants said, "Okay, yeah, okay, we won't cut it. We're just going to fix it so that *everybody* will notice it."

So Rat sat down on a log. And as he was sitting there all the ants came, and they were combing the hair on his tail. He had his tail sticking straight out, and they were combing it down just right. Pretty soon they got it all combed out.

Next they brought a string and tied it around the base of his tail. Then they sent for somebody else, even as they were whispering around.

"What are you whispering about?" the Rat demanded.

The Ants exclaimed, "Don't turn around! Don't look now! You're not supposed to look!" So the Rat turned back around.

And so they went on. Pretty soon the Ants came back and put a pine pitch, *sana*, on his tail while they were combing it. Then, when it was warm they would comb through it. Then they wrapped twine around his tail. And they kept wrapping twine around the Rat's tail until his whole tail was wrapped in the twine. And his hair was all wrapped up next to the tail. Then he said, "What are you guys doing back there? What are you doing to my tail?"

Rat started to turn and look, but the Ants said, "Don't look! You're going to ruin what we're doing!"

So the Rat turned back around . . . he was getting anxious. He was *so* anxious to look at his tail, and to see what they were doing.

Pretty soon they were finished. So the Rat turned around and looked—and saw his tail all wrapped up real nice and tight with that twine. Rat demanded, "*What* did you do to my tail?!"

The Ants said, "It's going to look *really*, *really* pretty. But you can't unwrap it until the day of the dance, until just a few minutes before the dance, when you're finally getting ready to go to the dance. *Then* you can unwrap your tail—and *everybody* is going to admire it." Then the Ants all walked away.

Ohhh, this was just *so hard* for Rat! It was hard for him to not know what they had done to his tail.

Finally, the day came when he was ready to take the twine off his tail. But when he pulled his tail around, he grabbed the end where they had the little knot tied, and he took that knot out. And when he started unwrapping his tail it started pulling all the hair out . . . "ouch, ouch, ouch, what did they do?!"

Rat kept pulling the twine out. But his hair kept getting stuck all over the twine. Finally, he got all the way down to the beginning of his tail. Rat just looked at all that pile of twine. And he looked at all of his beautiful hair that was stuck all over that piece of twine—and oh, he was mad! The Rat was enraged at the Ants for what they had done to his tail.

Rat looked at his tail again and *it was all bare*! There was no beautiful hair on his tail! Instead his tail was all scaly looking, where the pitch had dried up black, because they mixed it with black ashes from the fire. Now his tail was all black with little speckles all over it. And ever since this time Rats never have hair on their tail. It's all just skin or scales, and whatever else they have on their tail.

## LEGEND 18

# The Deer and the Antelope as Brothers

A *looong*, long time ago there were two brothers: the Deer and the Antelope. They traveled all over this land together. They went to the mountains and to the sage flats in search of food. They knew the best places to find green grass to eat. They went to all the springs in search of water. And at many springs there were places they could sleep and rest. The brothers were content, and happy to be together.

Then as time went on, the land started to dry up, and the clouds overhead passed them by without dropping any rain. A drought came upon the land.

One day Antelope told his brother, "I'm growing afraid. I don't think there is enough food for both of us on this land."

Deer answered, "You're right. Everywhere we go there is less and less grass."

Then Antelope inquired, "What should we do?"

After the brothers talked more about what was happening to the land, Deer told Antelope, "I think we have to split up and go our own way, or we may both starve!"

Sadly, Antelope agreed. "Yes," he said, "You are right."

Then Deer told his brother Antelope, "I will go to the mountains and live there. Maybe I will find food to eat there."

Antelope responded, "That's a good idea. I'll stay here, and see if I can find food to eat here in the sage and the prairie."

So they decided to do this, each to go his own way, so they would not end up fighting over any food they found together.

It was summer when the Deer went to the mountains. He was pleased when got there, and exclaimed, "I like this place! It has plenty of juniper trees for shade, and there are many places to rest and sleep. And there is a lot of green grass to eat." So the Deer was very happy in his new home.

Antelope was lonely after his brother Deer left. After a while Antelope decided it was time to travel once again over the land he knew as home. But as he moved along Antelope found that there were very few places where the grass was plentiful. Then one day Antelope decided that he would try and eat the bitterbrush, which was growing everywhere, all around him. So Antelope took a bite, and said, "Hmm . . . this tastes pretty good!"

Soon, bitterbrush was all that Antelope ate, and he was happy in his prairie home.

But as summer turned to fall Antelope missed his brother Deer, and thought to himself, "I wonder if my brother is still alive?" He thought sadly, "Surely he would have come to see me if he is."

That same day Deer was thinking about his brother, Antelope. And Deer was thinking to himself, "I wonder how Antelope is doing?"

The brothers Deer and Antelope were very lonesome for each other.

Deer decided to go look for his brother in the prairie. At the same time Antelope started to move toward the mountains to find his brother Deer. And as he traveled along Antelope thought, "I wonder if Deer is alive? And if he is I wonder if he will even remember me?"

So the Deer was going down the mountain to find his brother Antelope in the prairie, even as Antelope was moving to the mountain to find Deer.

Soon, Deer saw something in the distance and thought, "I wonder what that is?" Antelope saw something in the distance too, and thought, "I wonder what that is?" Both brothers were afraid that it might be a cougar in search of a meal.

As they got closer, however, Deer and Antelope finally recognized each other and started to run toward one another. They were glad to know that they were both still alive, and glad to see each other.

Excited, Antelope told his brother, "I was growing very, very sad, and thought you might have been killed, or died in the mountains. So I decided to come look for you."

After they visited for a while they decided to return to Antelope's home in the prairie. But they hadn't been there long before Deer said, "My brother, it is time for me to return to my home in the mountains, where I can eat grass."

Antelope sadly replied, "I will go with you to the foot of the mountain. But I cannot live in the mountains. I like it here, where there is plenty of bitterbrush and sunflower seed."

They agreed to leave on their journey together early the next morning, while it was still cool.

Early the next morning Deer thought to himself, "I wonder who is the fastest runner?" So he said to Antelope, "I think we should race to the foot of the mountains, to see who is fastest."

Antelope quickly agreed, "Okay!"

But before Antelope could even get ready Deer took off running. And as he bounced along he would look back at Antelope, trotting along behind. Deer teased, "Hurry, brother, you run like an old man! I thought you were supposed to be a fast runner!"

Then Deer continued to run as fast as he could, until Antelope was far behind and fading from sight.

Soon, Deer stopped on a little hill, and looked back to see where Antelope was. Then he shouted out, joking, "Hurry, my brother. Or I will eat up all the delicious green grass here at the foot of the mountains!"

But Antelope continued trotting along, and did not worry about his brother's teasing.

Then Deer took off once again, running as hard as he could.

But now Antelope was starting to catch up with Deer. So Antelope called out, "Brother you no longer run like a jack-rabbit. You run like an old toad!" Then Antelope laughed and continued on forward.

Eventually, Antelope looked up, and saw that the sun was starting to make it hot in the prairie. So he slowed down.

Soon, Deer called back to him, saying, "I am thirsty," and asking, "Where is the spring in this vast land? I want to know so I can get a drink of water."

Antelope teased his brother, saying, "It's at the foot of the mountain, so you better hurry."

So Deer continued on his way. But Antelope soon caught up with him, and said, "Why are you running so . . . *slow*?" You are not jumping high over the brush, like you did at the beginning." And Antelope continued to tease Deer, "Hurry, Hurry, before it gets too hot! Oh, just imagine . . . that *nice, coool* water in the spring, there at the foot of the mountains! Hurry, Hurry!"

Now Deer spoke out with anger, "It's too hot to be running. The distance is too long!" Deer was not happy anymore. So he murmured, "Now, let's rest and visit for a while."

"No!" Antelope explained. "I always go until I reach the land I am looking for!" So, Antelope continued on without his brother.

When Deer finally reached the spring of cool water in the foothills of the mountains, Antelope was already there. Antelope had already drunk from the cool water of the spring and was taking a little nap in the shade of the trees.

Deer was hot and tired and angry when he finally arrived at the cool spring.

Since that time, Antelope and Deer have lived apart from one another. Antelope is happy to live in the flat, open country of the desert, with bitterbrush all around. And Deer is pleased to live in the mountains, with cool springs and green grasses and shade and shelter all around.

On occasion, you will still see the brothers eating together there in the foothills, visiting and talking about the old days. But they don't race and play tricks on each other anymore.

## LEGEND 19

# Obsidian and Rock, Deer and Coyote

A *looong*, long time ago, there were four friends who traveled all over this land together. They were the rock and obsidian, and the Coyote and the Deer. They did *everything* together when they were on this land. The Deer and the Coyote were fast and could travel quickly, so they would go up into the mountains together. But the obsidian and the rock stayed down in the flat lands and the basins, because they weren't as fast as Coyote and Deer.

One day the four friends were sitting by the campfire and talking about receiving their power. And while they were talking one of the rocks said, "In order to receive your power, you have to have a dream. So everybody has to dream when they're asleep tonight. Then the power that's going to take care of us is going to come to you and give you a song. So that's what we should do tonight when we all go to sleep. We should all try to have a good dream. Then maybe we'll become very powerful friends, and able to help other people with whatever power we have."

They all agreed. "Yeah, okay, that's sounds good," they said, as they sat around the fire. Finally, the fire started to die down, so they all decided to go to sleep. Then they all went to sleep and slept throughout the night.

Obsidian started to dream, and knew right away what this dream was all about.

Then the rock dreamed, and saw what he was going to become.

The Deer had a dream, too. But Deer had a bad dream. And it scared him, because he didn't know what to think about it. So he started turning this way and that way in his sleep. Then he woke up and looked at his friends, who were still asleep. So the Deer lay back down and went back to sleep.

Coyote had his dream, too, but he also had a bad dream. So Coyote started tossing and turning back and forth saying, "No, no, no!" He also woke up briefly and looked around at his friends. But they were all still asleep. He looked around the fire. It was just barely going, and the smoke was coming up from it. Coyote closed his eyes again, and lay there for a while. Then the sun came up, so he sat up.

"Okay, guys," he said, "it's time to get up." So they all sat up and started looking around. They were stretching their arms and rubbing their eyes and starting to shake off the sleep and move around. "Well," Coyote said, "who wants to be the first one to share their dream?"

Obsidian said, "I had a really good dream last night. I dreamed I became very, very powerful, and that I was *flying* through the air! My brother Deer saw me coming and ran away, because he feared my power. But I hit the deer. And when I hit the deer my power was so strong that he just fell over." Obsidian liked the dream, but it made the Deer fearful.

Then the rock spoke up and said, "I had a similar dream." He went on, "I also dreamed that I was *flying* through the air! My brother, Coyote, saw me coming. But I was moving too fast, so I flew on in and hit him in the head. When I hit Coyote in the head, it knocked him down!" Rock liked the dream and the story, but Coyote didn't.

Coyote looked down at the ground and the embers of the fire, thinking. Then he turned around and grabbed a stick that was lying there on the ground. It was a stick they used to poke the fire. Then he started hitting the rock with the stick and said, "I had a bad dream last night. I dreamed I was busting this rock into pieces!" Then he plucked the rock up off the ground, and knocked it all to pieces, into small, little pieces of gravel. Then the deer jumped up and started pawing at the obsidian, and busted it all to pieces, too. Then Coyote and Deer looked at one another and then ran off in different directions. They were never friends again after that.

So to this day, our people have used obsidian to make arrow points to hunt the deer. And still today it works well. And whenever the coyotes come too close to our camp, all we have to do is bend over and pretend to pick up some rocks. Then you lift them over your head, like you're going to throw—and coyote will run off, too. From that time on, our people hunted with obsidian points and shattered rocks. But Coyote and Deer were never friends again.

# First Woman Travels in Search of Her Husband . . . and Is Followed by a Skull and Bones

Long, long ago, after the first man and first woman were created, they became separated from one another. The man went off roaming the world to see what was across the land. And the woman stayed behind and took care of the household and brought in things to survive on. But with the passage of time she became lonely for somebody to talk to. Then she thought to herself, "I wonder if something happened to my husband. Maybe he got hurt someplace and needs my help. Maybe I should go look for him, to see if I can find him."

So she decided to go look for her husband. She put a large basket, a *kawona*, on her back. She packed her possessions and food there, to keep her over. And she filled her water bottle, *paosa*. Then she started out in the direction her husband had traveled.

The first day she traveled along and looked everywhere. When she got on top of a hill she looked as far out as she could see. She saw no signs of her mate. Then she made camp and ate part of her food.

The next day she changed directions and went a different way. Once again she traveled all day. When she came upon a small hill, she would look out across the land to see if she could see any sign of her husband. She traveled this way for a *long* time.

One day while she was traveling she came upon a Meadowlark that was injured. As she was walking past, the Meadowlark pleaded softly, "Please stop. Please help me." The woman felt sorry for the little bird and picked it up. That's when she saw that it had a broken wing. So she fixed its wing. She broke off a little twig of rabbit brush and with her obsidian knife scraped the bark off. With sinew thread she tied the twig onto the wing, and thus fixed the broken wing!

To repay the kindness of the woman Meadowlark told her, "Whatever it is that you want to know, ask me and I'll tell you what I know."

So the woman asked Meadowlark, "Have you seen a man traveling through this land all by himself? I'm looking for him. That's my husband. And I'm afraid he might have gotten hurt and can't come back home."

Meadowlark told her, "You're going in the right direction. Just keep going the way you are headed, and you'll come to a little creek. Follow that creek up into the hills. When you get to the bottom of the hills you're going to see some bones lying next to the rocks." Meadowlark warned her, "Don't touch them! Don't bother them. Just leave them alone and go on past them, and keep following the creek."

The woman started out again and traveled until it got dark. Then she made her camp. The next morning she woke up and had a little more to eat and again went on her way. She could see the hills in the distance and she kept moving toward them.

When she got close to the hills she saw the bones piled up neatly on the ground. She went over and looked at them and thought to herself, "I wonder why Meadowlark told me to leave these bones alone? It looks like they've been here for a *long*, long time."

She turned around and found a dry limb from a tree. Then she went back to the bones and stuck the limb in the eye socket of the skull, and moved the bones all around. Then she stood there and thought, "Nothing happened!"

So she put the bones back with the stick and then started walking again. She started walking up into the hills. Then she went a different direction, and went the way that she was told.

When she started going down the other side of the hill she heard a noise, "Chuh, chuh, chuh, chuh, chuh, chuh!" She turned around and looked behind her, but couldn't see anything. So she turned around and started to walk again. Then she heard it once again, "Chuh, chuh, chuh, chuh, chuh!" She turned around and looked back once more, but again she didn't see anything. So she kept on going.

Then she came upon Ground Squirrel's house and said, "I was told to come in this direction. A long time ago my husband left me, and he never came back. But Meadowlark told me how to find him, so that's what I'm doing."

Ground Squirrel told her, "I know where your husband is. You're going the right way." Then he scolded her, "But you were told to leave those bones alone. You were told to leave them alone, but you moved them!"

She replied, "No, I didn't! I didn't bother them! I saw them and I walked on past them."

Ground Squirrel said, "No, you disturbed them. That is why they are following you."

They parted ways and the woman continued in the direction Ground Squirrel told her to go. When the sun went down she again made a camp. The next morning when she got ready to leave she heard that noise again: "Chuh, chuh, chuh, chuh, chuh." She turned around to look and thought, "It sounds like it's getting close to me." So she started walking faster!

As she moved ahead she came to the place at the edge of a big lake where Ground Squirrel had told her to make a house out of willows and cattail leaves. So she cut the willows and made a frame. And she gathered the cattail leaves, and fixed them and put them over the frame to form her house.

Above the lake there was *ebe*, a kind of white chalk. So she got the *ebe* and painted her house all white, because that's what Ground Squirrel had told her to do. Then she went inside and closed the door, a door that was also made out of cattails.

When she closed the door she again heard that noise coming closer, "Chuh, chuh, chuh, chuh, chuh, chuh, chuh!" Ground Squirrel had warned her, "You're going to hear those bones getting close, but *don't peek out*! Whatever you do, *don't* peek out!"

She heard the sound getting very close. And pretty soon she heard: "CHUH!" She heard something hit the side of the house, "chuh, chuh, chuh." And then, "CHUH!" on the opposite side of the house. Again she heard, "chuh, chuh, chuh, chuh, chuh! CHUH!" And, ohhh, she really wanted to look out to see what was happening. But she kept thinking, "I was told not to be curious, not to look outside."

The skull hit the house one more time, and then things became quiet . . . And the woman got scared, because she didn't know what was happening outside. She really wanted to look outside. But she waited and waited and waited. Finally, she thought, "Well, I'm going to look out." So she opened the door. And when she opened the door and peeked out there was no skull, there were no more bones.

She stayed there for one night. But her food was getting very low, for she had eaten almost all of it. So she said to herself, "Ground Squirrel said I would find an Old Lady living all by herself."

She went in the direction that she had been told. And she came upon a cattail house like the one she had made. But there was nobody home. Next to the cattail house was a *haba* frame, which they used to dry fish or deer meat, and all kinds of food. Then she knew somebody was living there. So she decided to wait, thinking, "I'll just wait for them to come home."

Toward evening she heard someone coming. She heard the footsteps. She became frightened, thinking it might be the bones again. But it was Old Lady Swan coming home, carrying Groundhogs she had killed. "I'm glad to see you," the woman said to Old Lady Swan, and went on to explain, "I was told to come here and that I would find your home here. So I've been waiting for you."

Old Lady Swan sat down and looked at the woman and said in a low voice, "I knew you were going to be here, so I brought food for us to cook." She fixed the ashes in the fire and cooked two of the Groundhogs, and hung the others up on the *haba*. Then she cooked two of them, one for her and one for the traveler, and they ate together.

Then Old Lady Swan told the woman, "Well, you come in here, come inside to sleep." So she made a place for the woman to sleep, and the woman slept inside.

The next morning the woman woke up and Old Lady Swan was gone. The woman was worried again, because she didn't have a chance to ask where her husband was or how to find him. So she waited again.

Toward evening Old Lady Swan came back again. This time she had ducks, Mallard Ducks. So she hung them on one of the posts of the *haba* and then cooked two of them over the fire—one for herself and one for her visitor. Then it got dark and they sat around the fire.

While they were talking the woman told Old Lady Swan, "A long time ago, my husband left to go see what the faraway land was like, but he never came back. I fear he might have been hurt, and he might need my help. So I've been looking for him, trying to find him."

Old Lady Swan told her, "I know where he stays. But you get rest tonight and tomorrow you'll go there."

*Ohhh* . . . the woman became very, *very* happy, because finally she knew her journey was coming to an end.

The next morning Old Lady Swan was still there. She hadn't gone out hunting as usual. Then Old Lady Swan told the woman, "You go beyond those hills, way over there," she pointed, "in that direction." She was pointing south as the way to go. "You're going to come to a big mountain and from there you'll see the smoke from his fire. That's where he's at. That's where you're going to find him."

In preparation the woman filled up her water bottle and took some of the dry meat that was hanging up and that was given to her by the Old Lady Swan. Then she went toward the big mountain Old Lady Swan had pointed out to her.

As she traveled the woman came to a big hill, and from there she could see the distant mountains. And she could see smoke going up from a distant campfire! She was very, very happy, because she knew that soon she would be back with her husband again.

She started walking faster. Then she would get tired and stop for a while. And then she would walk fast again. She was getting closer and closer and closer. Finally, she found her husband and they were back together again. Her kindness to Meadowlark and her devotion to her husband had been rewarded.

# A Legend of Darker- and Lighter-Skinned Children—and Prophesies of White People Coming Out of the East

After the first couple were together for a while, the woman got pregnant and had a little boy. The little boy was dark-skinned, the same way the parents were, and they raised him in the tribe. Later, she gave birth to a little girl. The little girl had light hair, and her skin was also light. As the children grew they fought with one another until the mother and father would separate them.

The father taught the boy how to hunt, how to fish, how to make arrowheads, how to make spears, how to make fish hooks, how to make twine for nets—all the things that a young man needed to know. The mother tried very earnestly to teach the girl how to gather and split willows, how to make baskets, how to weave other things, how to tan hides for clothing, how to sew moccasins, how to grind pine nuts—all those things a young woman needed to know. But the girl had a hard time listening.

As time went on the woman had another little girl. And this little girl was dark-skinned with black hair. When she got older her mother started teaching her the same things: how to sew, how to tan hides, how to grind food, how to dig roots, and so on. And the younger little girl learned all of those things.

With the passage of time the woman had another little boy. This little boy had light skin and light-colored hair. The father tried to teach him how to make nets and how to make arrow-heads and how to hunt and how to fish. But the little boy acted like his mind was far away. He never learned a lot of things like the first boy.

One day when the children appeared to be playing they were actually fighting. And one of the boys shot the arrow and that hit the father's leg while he was sleeping. The father woke up and was *very* angry. And he knew immediately that he had to do something because his four children weren't getting along. The two dark-skinned children got along real well, and the two light-skinned children also got along well with each other.

So the father a got a *mukuna*, a magical stick. With the stick he picked up the two light-skinned children and threw them *way* across a big lake toward the east. As they were fly-ing through the air he called out to them, "One day you'll find your way back here to your home." Then he told the two children that he had left, "Your brother and sister will come back again someday."

As time went on the children still with the family multiplied and became more and more and more numerous, to the way it is today.

Then, many generations later, there was a time when the word came from Indians in the east. They said that the light-skinned people were coming back to our land. And at that time there was a really great chief and leader of the Paiute people. And that chief knew all the stories from the past.

So he called the people together and he told them, "Our brothers and sisters are coming back. This was foretold from our past people. One day they're going to come back to our land. And if I'm alive, we're going to go to meet them. But if I die, I want you to remember that they're our brothers and sisters from long, long ago."

When that chief was a very old man the people saw covered wagons coming across the land and out of the dust. This was somewhere down by Winnemucca in Nevada or Lovelock, Nevada. And these were covered wagons being pulled by oxen. Then the word came that the light-skinned people were coming back!

So the old chief called the people together and said, "We have to go meet our brothers and sisters." So they went out to meet them. They brought dried deer meat. And they killed some ducks and brought some ducks. They brought that kind of food and went to meet the people arriving, because that's the way our people were—always sharing food with visitors. So they went out to meet the light-skinned people, finally coming home.

When they were getting close to them, those white people, these light-skinned people, got their guns and shot at them! So the Indians retreated up into the hills to get away from the wagons that were coming.

Then that great old leader, in his retreat, lost one of his moccasins. So they used to call him *One-ah-mucca*, meaning one moccasin—and then that name got corrupted into Winnemucca.

So that is how Chief Winnemucca, a first chief of the people, got his name in battle. And this is what happened when the people went out to meet their light-skinned brothers and sisters coming out of the dust. This is how the story was told to me.

# Comments on Rock Art— "Coyote Writing" and "Spiritual Writing" in Paiute Country

When I was a child, and as I grew up, I spent a considerable amount of time with my grandma and grandpa. We drove on a lot of the roads in Central Oregon long before they were ever paved. And sometimes we would take shortcuts on our way to Prineville or Powell Butte, or on our way to Burns or to Beatty, Oregon. During those travels, my grandma and grandpa would share stories about the land, about the lakes, the hills and the lava beds and caves. And they would show old trails where the Paiute people used to cross the desert.

They would also point out where there were springs, and where there was good drinking water. And when they were saying that they used to put it this way, "Maybe one day when you grow up, you might get stuck out here in the desert. Then you'll remember that there's water over here, just out of sight. That's where our people always got water. There's an old campsite over there."

They even pointed out and shared where there were burials sites, what you would call historic burial sites. These ancient sites were already here when our people, my Paiute people, would come into Central Oregon from the Warm Spring Reservation. They'd come down to the Bend area or to the La Pine area to hunt. And they went to Sisters, and over to

Paulina. They went to these places to go hunting, and to gather berries or to dig the different roots used by our people. My people liked to come back to our ancient homeland.

So my grandma and grandpa would talk about those burials, who the person was and where they were buried. That went on for a long time, while I was a little boy. When I became a teenager, and after my grandpa passed away, I started taking my grandma on trips with me. As we traveled I would ask her about those stories I heard while I was growing up. I was always asking, "Where did that happen?" or "What's over by that mountain again?" or "What did you guys say was over there?" Then my grandma would tell and retell the stories. She would name the names of major land features in Paiute.

### "Coyote Writing" in Paiute Country

It was at that time, and during those long trips and long hours of storytelling, that I learned about the petroglyphs and pictographs that are all over Central and Eastern Oregon. This was the land that my grandma called, "Paiute country."

Later, as I got older, I went in search of those places and examples of rock art that my grandparents (and my teachers) had pointed out to me. And I found many of the pictographs and petroglyphs that my grandma told the stories about, and that my grandpa told stories about. Our people call those writings on the rock *etsatubono*, which means, literally, "Coyote writings." But this suggests not so much that our people believe that Coyote wrote them, as it is reference to their age. In our Paiute traditions and legends, the animal people were put into this world before human beings. So our reference to Coyote writings is intended to suggest that those writings and images are ancient, and were made by the first creation.

Also, this rock art is part of the history of my people as an ancient people, and a testimonial to my people's survival on this land. Rock art images are often found in special places. Sometimes they're up in the mountains. Sometimes they're at the edge of a stream or lake. Sometimes they're up in an inaccessible place along the rimrock, overlooking a canyon or the land. And sometimes they're right next to a village site.

There are some examples of Coyote writing that are so extensive you can't count them all, because they take up so much room. There are places on the rimrock where there's not a boulder or a flat surface that doesn't have something written on it. It's that way down in the Hart Mountain area in southeast Oregon. But there are also lone figures, one figure on a boulder, out in the middle of the desert, and you'll never find another pictograph or petroglyph within twenty to fifty miles of that one lone figure.

These Coyote writings are not something that was written by just anybody. They are very sacred writings. In the past, for our people like many tribes, only the holy people, sometimes known as medicine men or Indian doctors, only they held the right to have the red paint used in a lot of these writings. Even more rare are the writings with white paint or black paint or even yellow paint. These were ceremonial paints. Among the Paiute people the general population of the various bands knew where to gather these paints. But because of their sacredness not everybody kept them. So wherever there are such writings was a holy place for our people, because something happened there that caused the holy people to make that mark, recording that event.

In the dry river canyon east of Bend there is a well-known site of sacred figures. One is called *Patusuwadyadu*. That means a dying star. According to the stories I learned, that writing recorded a time when a meteorite came down somewhere down south, in the Klamath country or in northern California. It hit the earth and made smoke and dust go up so thick that it killed a lot of animals and people. There are also figures of deer, because the mule deer was a major source of food for the survival of our people. When young men were getting to the point in their life to become hunters they were sent to some of the places where there are sacred writings. There they would fast and pray, and ask for the good fortune to become a good hunter. And there are areas up around Mount Bachelor and Three Sisters that have elk drawings, because some of our hunters went after the elk in the mountains. And there are the drawings of some people of the desert. There are representations of snakes and lizards and water bugs, and even those writings and images that people call mythical creatures. Well, among our people, even to this day, there's a few of us left that believe in the reality of those creatures. They've never left here. They're still here.

These are the things that make those sites holy. It really causes me deep anguish when I visit sites that have been vandalized, sometimes with spray paint, charcoal, or white chalk. people have put their initials on these sacred rocks, and the dates when they were there. Sometimes they try to reproduce some of the drawings. To the Indian people that's very disrespectful, because to us those holy places are just like a cathedral or a church. They're just like an archive you might find at the Vatican or in the Smithsonian. They tell a story about the people that were here—and the people that are still here. It's part of our continuing history.

Some of those writings are boundary markers. They mark the boundaries of the Northern Paiute people and the lands that belong to us, that the creator gave us. That's why it was important to my grandparents to pass on this information to us. And part of the teaching was to always remember the sacredness of life, and to remember when the deer and the elk, the squirrels, the groundhogs, the fish, whatever kind of a life, to remember when the animal people were the first people on the world. Later they became our food, food for the human people. And there are lines in the rock, lines that everybody has their own ideas about. Some of the lines represent the root foods. And some of the lines represent the medicines that our people used, medicines that are found in the area of those sacred writings. To me, it's almost like a prescription, for we still use those plants and medicines today.

But a lot of this knowledge has been lost. I have white friends that have been very good to me, friends that have found these sites, and found the best and easiest way to get to them. And when we visit the sites and we've sat there, I've meditated and looked out over the land surrounding those sacred writings. And almost, it comes into your mind, comes in to your heart, why those writings were and are at that exact place. And for me, as an Indian person, your heart just, like, jumps because you realize why your people made those marks in that particular place. And I've been to places where there's been a certain kind of plant you can't find at any other place. And there's a spring nearby, and maybe those figures are the little people that live in the water, in the springs. Or maybe a healing took place there, or somebody's life was saved there, or a baby was born there.

All of these things are part of these writings, all across our ancient homeland in the desert. They show how sacred this land is to the Indian people, to our people. So it's important to leave these sacred drawings alone, not only for my people, but for all people. These writings are just a little bit of our story that everyone, no matter the color of their skin, should have respect for. So people should leave these sacred writings as they are, because they are there for a reason.

We don't like people marking on the rocks that have a story, because they're disrupting the story of that land. Maybe there will come a time in the future when the rocks will talk to us again through these writings, and help prepare us for the future. But right now that knowledge is asleep. That's why it's important for everybody to respect the writings as something holy. They deserve the same respect as the cave art in Europe that everybody writes about, telling the stories of the cavemen that wrote through these pictures and images. There are similar and sacred rock art writings in Asia, in the Himalayas, and in Russia and elsewhere. All of these sites are sacred and protected. But sometimes in the United States we have all the laws to protect these sacred writings and places, but people still continue to deface and destroy them. They may sit on public land and belong to all of us. But even if the land is private, that doesn't give anyone the right to destroy our sacred Coyote writings. They should be left alone for everybody to enjoy, and at some time to help us to understand who we are and where we come from.

# Glossary

*Agi* – Salmon
*atsa* – an edible seed
*dosa* – medicinal plant
*ebe* – white mineral paint; sacred paint
*Etsa'a* – Coyote
*etsatubono* – Coyote writings
*haape* – desert parsley
*haba* – shade made out of willows
*kangedya* – bitterroot
*kawona* – burden basket made of willows
*Kedu* – Groundhog
*Koepa* – Bighorn Sheep
*moohedu* – leader
*mukuna* – magical stick or staff
*Mu naa'a* – our father
*Nuwu* – what the Northern Paiute call tribe
*Nuwuddu* – ancient people
*Nuwuzo'ho* – cannibal
*One-ah-mucca* – original word that was corrupted to
    Winnemucca
*Pahizoho'o* – giant
*paosa* – water bottle
*pappe* – pine nut soup

*Patusuwadyadu* – dying star; falling star
*sana* – pine pitch
*Saya* – Mud Hen
*tamano* – spring season
*tatza* – summer season
*Tekawa* – Rat; Wood Rat
*tomo* – winter season
*tseabu* – wild rose bush
*tsuga* – desert parsley
*Tuhudya* – Mule Deer
*Tukwahane* – Paiute name of sacred butte; a.k.a. Castle Rock
*wea* – rabbit skin blanket
*Weyawewa* – name of Paiute chief
*wye* – rice grass, an edible plant
*yabano* – fall season
*yapa* – Indian carrot
*Yapatikadu* – name of Paiute band, Indian Carrot Eaters

# Recommended Reading

Aguilar, George. 2005. *When the River Ran Wild! Indian Traditions on the Mid-Columbia and the Warm Springs Reservation.* Portland: Oregon Historical Society Press.

Alexander, Hartley Burr. 2005. *Native American Mythology.* New York: Dover Publications.

Clark, Ella. 1953. *Indian Legends of the Pacific Northwest,* Berkeley: University of California Press.

Clark, Ella. 1955. "George Gibbs' Account of Indian Mythology in Oregon and Washington Territories." *Oregon Historical Quarterly* 56(4): 293–325.

Cressman, Luther. 1962. *The Sandal and the Cave.* CITY: Champoeg Press.

Curtin, Jeremiah and Edward Sapir. 1909. *Wishram texts,* Late E. J. Brill, Layton: Publishers and Printers (Ulan Press, 2014 reprint).

Dixon, Roland. 1911. "Shasta Myths." *Journal of American Folklore 23.*

Guie, Eister Dean Ed. 1990. *Coyote Stories.* Lincoln: University of Nebraska Press.

Herman, Ruth. 1972. *The Paiutes of Pyramid Lake.*

Hines, Donald M. 1991. *The Forgotten Tribes, Oral Tales of the Teninos and Mid-Columbia River Indian Nations.*

Hittman, Michael. 1990. *Wavoka and The Ghost Dance.*

Hopkins, Sarah Winnemucca. 1883. *Life Among the Paiutes: Their Wrongs and Claims.* Bishop: Chalfant Press, Inc.

Inter-Tribal Council of Nevada. 1976. *Numa: A Northern Paiute History*. SLC: University of Utah Printing Service.

Johnson, Edward C. 1975. *Walker River Paiutes: A Tribal History*, SLC: University of Utah Printing Service.

Judson, Katharine Berry. 1997. *Myths and Legends of the Pacific Northwest*. Lincoln: University of Nebraska Press.

Karson, Jennifer, et al. eds. 2006. *wiyaxayxt as days go by wiyaakaa? Awn: Our History, Our Land, and Our People: The Cayuse, Umatilla and Walla Walla*. Pendleton and Portland: Tamastslikt Cultural Institute and Oregon Historical Society.

Kelly, Isabel. 1932. "Ethnography of the Surprise Valley Paiutes." *University of California Publications in American Archeology and Ethnography* 31.

Kelly, Isabel. 1938. "Northern Paiute Tales." *The Journal of American Folklore* 51: 202.

Kehoe, Alice Beck. 2006. *The Ghost Dance: Ethnohistory & Revitalization*, Second Edition. Long Grove: Waveland Press, Inc.

Lyman, W. D. 1904. "Myths and Superstition of the Oregon Indians." *American Antiquarian Society*.

Lowie, Robert. 1909. "The Northern Shoshone." *Anthropological Papers of the American Museum of Natural History* 2.

Mackey, Harold and Thomas Brundage. 1968. "Á Molale Indian Myth of Coyote." *Northwest Folklore 3*, no.2 Winter.

Mardsen, W. L. 1923. "The Northern Paiute Language of Oregon." *University of California Publications in American Archaeology and Ethnology* 20.

Mooney, James. 1973. *The Ghost Dance Religion and Wounded Knee*. New York: Dover Publications.

George Peter Murdock. 1938. "Notes on the Tenino, Molala, and Paiute of Oregon." In *American Anthropologist*, N.S., 40: 396.

Palmer, William R. 1946. *Pahute Indian Legends*. SLC, Utah: Desert Book Company.

Ramsey, Jarold. 1977. *Coyote Was Going There: Indian Literature of the Oregon Country*. Seattle: University of Washington Press.

Ramsey, Jarold. 1972. "Three Wasco-Warm Springs Stories." *Western Folklore* 31 (April).

Ray, Verne. 1939. "Tribal Distribution in Eastern Oregon and Adjacent Regions." *American Anthropologist* 40.

Ruby, Robert H. and John A. Brown, *Dreamer Prophets of the Columbia Plateau* (1989)

Slickpoo, Allen. 1972. *Nu Mee Poom Tit Wah Tit: Nez Perce Tales.* Lapwai: Nez Perce Tribes of Idaho.

Spier, Leslie and Edward Sapir. 1930. *Wishram Ethnography.* Seattle: University of Washington Press (Publications in Anthropology 3:3).

Spinden, Herbert. 1908. "Myths of the Nez Perce Indians." *Journal of American Folklore* 21.

Steward, Julian. 1970. "The Foundation of Basin-Plateau Shoshonean Society." In *Languages and Cultures of Western North America*, edited by Earl H. Swanson Jr. Pocatello: Idaho State University Press.

Stowell, Cynthia D. 1951. *Faces of a Reservation —A Portrait of the Warm Springs Indian Reservation.*

Trejo, Judy. http://tv.powwows.com/video/2012/07/20/paiute-native-american-shaman-wovoka-and-the-ghost-dance/.

Trejo, Judy. 1974. "Coyote Tales: A Paiute Commentary." *The Journal of American Folklore* 87 (343).

Walker Jr., Deward E., et. al. 1994. *Nez Perce Coyote Tales: The Myth Cycle.* Norman: University of Oklahoma Press.

Wheat, Margaret. 1967. *Survival Arts of the Primitive Paiutes.*

Wheeler-Voegelin, Ermine. 1955. "The Northern Paiutes of Central Oregon." *Ethnohistory* 2 (2).

Whiting, Beatrice B. 1950. *Paiute Sorcery.* New York: Viking Fund Publications.